Zombie Ever After

Byzantium Sky Press
Ellendale, DE 19941

First Byzantium Sky Press ebook edition, October 2024
First Byzantium Sky Press paperback edition, December 2024
First Printing 2021

Cover Design by Crystal Heidel, Byzantium Sky Press
Cover artwork by Dark Queen Designs

ISBN 978-1-955872-25-6 (ebook)
ISBN 978-1-955872-24-9 (paperback)

Library of Congress Control Number: 2024946051

For information, address Byzantium Sky Press, 26119 Beacon Drive, Ellendale, DE 19941 or email byzantiumskypress@gmail.com.

Manufactured and Printed in the United States of America

LIZ DEJESUS

BYZANTIUM
Sky Press

PROLOGUE

Neve ran through the woods. For some reason, no matter how fast she ran, it felt as though she was running through quicksand. Her lungs burned from the exertion, yet she was going nowhere fast. From the ground beneath her feet, something grabbed her ankle. She screamed, falling face first to the ground. Turning quickly onto her back, she watched in horror as her mother, Violet, crawled out of the pitch-black soil, her rotten hand tightly gripping Neve's ankle.

Her mother's tan skin became the color of ashes. Her dark brown eyes turned blood red. Her luscious black hair vanished, leaving nothing but a matted and patchy scalp.

"Mom! Please don't do this," Neve pleaded as she pushed herself away from her mother's advances.

Her father, Charles, appeared and tackled Violet to the ground, keeping her away from their daughter.

"Run, Neve! Run!" he shouted.

"Daddy, look out!" she cried as her mother plunged her decayed teeth into her father's shoulder.

"Run!" he said, continuing to fight off his wife.

"Daddy!" Neve screamed as she sat up and gasped. Her baby blue pajamas and white bed sheets were drenched with cold sweat.

She'd had the nightmare again.

There was no response to her cry.

"Daddy! Daddy, where are you?" Neve shouted into the darkness that filled her room. Despite the darkness, the stars and constellations that her mother had glued to the ceiling glowed in the dark with a soft, ethereal green light.

She heard a loud, long moan from the end of the hallway. Her father's bedroom was in that direction. She frowned but pulled her dagger out of the sheath wrapped around her thigh. Neve instinctively readied her weapon just like he'd taught her.

Could there have been a security breach?

Impossible.

The Orchard, their compound, was impenetrable. The old building that once upon a time had been someone's castle was now fortified thanks to Charles and his team of brilliant architects and construction workers. Hidden in a remote location in the Rocky Mountains, the compound was secure. Her father had made certain it could never be accessed without a code. He'd made all the modifications himself. It was one reason they'd survived the virus.

Aetervia.

It started out as a chemical that would help people stay younger, but there were side effects from a bad batch.

Ash colored skin.

Blood red eyes.

Insatiable hunger for blood and flesh. Decaying flesh. All it took was a single bite for the infection to take hold of someone.

Millions had died.

Men.

Women.

Children.

"Neve . . . NEVE!" A loud moan quickly followed the haunting call of her name. There was no doubt about it; her father needed help.

Neve ran to her father's room, stopping at the reinforced door to punch in the code.

VINE7.

The door slid open with a soft hiss, and she stepped inside. Neve scanned the room for a moment and immediately found her father lying beside his large bed.

"No!"

He was on the floor, writhing in agony. His skin was pale. His once vibrant green eyes were reddish brown and vacant. His chocolate brown hair had lost its shine. She ran to his side and knelt.

"How did this happen?" she demanded.

"Ungh . . . L–L–Liiii . . . Lila . . ." He gurgled.

Neve frowned. Her stepmother Lila had been acting strange lately, spending more and more time in her laboratory doing God knew what. Neve took a quick look around to be certain that Lila wasn't anywhere in the room.

"Where is she?"

"G–gone," Charles replied. His eyes slowly changed to a deep blood red. That could only mean one thing.

Neve's heart dropped to her stomach. "Oh God. Daddy, please don't go. Don't leave me here," she whispered.

"Kill . . . me." He whimpered as he broke into a cold sweat, his body convulsing.

Neve shook her head.

"Do it!" he shouted, his skin turning ashen gray. His cheeks sunk, and his skin flaked off.

It was already too late.

She found her father's machete leaning against the wall next to the bed. Within reach, as always. She held the wooden hilt, soft and worn from years of use, and lifted the blade. She was always surprised by its lightness. That was why her father loved the machete. He could hack and slash all day long and not be sore. Now it was hers.

"I love you."

He growled at her in response. *He* was already gone.

Before Neve had a moment to second guess herself, she brought the blade down right on her father's neck with expert precision. She had been trained to know exactly where to kill a zombie. She knew every bone, artery, and muscle on the human body. Right between the mandibula and the clavicula. It was easy for her to be scientific about this because the creature before her was no longer her father. This was a monster now.

Warm blood splattered all over her chest and neck. She didn't even flinch when she felt the blood drip down to her belly. Neve would burn his body and her dirty, bloodied clothes later. There was no way of knowing if the virus had mutated and was now being transmitted through contact with blood. Her father's body twitched a few times before going still.

Neve dropped the machete as though it had burned her; it fell to the carpeted floor with a soft thud.

Her father was dead. She had expected to feel devastated, lonely, angry . . . something, anything. But all she felt was numb. As if every single emotion she had ever felt left her soul and forgot to leave something behind.

She had no frame of reference for this. Her mother had died when she was a toddler. All she remembered about her mother was that she loved to laugh and that she had kind brown eyes that always crinkled when she smiled. The funeral was a blur . . . an ocean of black clothing and sad faces all around.

Neve had no idea what the right or wrong way to grieve was . . . if there even was such a thing. She kept waiting for a dark ocean to flood the room and take her away. But nothing ever came. Only silence.

ONE

NEVE TUCKED HER JET-BLACK HAIR BEHIND HER EARS AND BLEW soft kisses in the air. She had been crouched in the same position for a while now, and her legs burned something fierce. But she wasn't going to move any time soon.

"Come here, little bunny. I won't hurt you," Neve whispered sweetly.

It was a small rabbit. Light brown with a pink nose that twitched as it sniffed the carrot Neve had placed as bait. It was probably the runt of the litter, either that or it was starving. Neve took a deep breath and forced her aching body to sit still even though all she wanted to do was kick the tree behind her in frustration. The bunny was taking way too long to warm up to her. Neve was being patient and gentle, all the usual crap that worked on most animals.

Then finally, after what felt like an eternity, the rabbit hopped forward and closed in on the minuscule carrot. It was the only one they had grown in their poor excuse of a garden, so Neve had cut it up into several pieces and used it as bait for the animals in the sparse forest.

Things had changed over the last ten years. There was once plenty of game and greenery all around their compound. But with each passing year, things had changed, and they were left to scavenge what little they could find.

Neve grinned when the rabbit was within her reach. In a flash, she leapt forward and had the bunny by the scruff of its neck. She snapped its neck with a soft crack before it could offer any form of struggle.

"Bunny stew . . . is what's for dinner." Neve stuffed her prize in the emerald-green sack. It would keep the other rabbit and the quail company. Neve pushed a blue button on her shoulder and called back her seven search droids. She worked with them every day to make sure there weren't any zombies in the area while she searched for clean water and uninfected game. Last thing she and her friends needed was to get sick from food. Or worse. So far, the only way to get infected with the Aetervia virus was by getting bitten by someone or something. But they would rather be safe than sorry.

Rather than carry a shotgun, which would blast an animal's head into little chunks, she preferred a small-caliber rifle to kill anything from a squirrel to a deer while preserving as much meat as possible. For close-range, she carried her father's machete. And for good measure, she also brought a collection of throwing knives, shuriken, and whatever else she could get her hands on.

She had created a makeshift armor for herself. All of the bulletproof vests were too big for her petite frame. With a diamond cutter, she had cut several pieces of an old piece of armor that no one was using and made herself a chest plate that fit her perfectly. She made sure she never had any parts of her body exposed except for her face. She had tried wearing a helmet, but it limited her vision too much. At least the rest of her body was protected.

She had also fashioned herself a long sleeve shirt out of aramid fabric. It was bulletproof as well, but the main reason she wore it was in case she had a one-on-one encounter with a zombie. It was the best way to avoid getting bitten and infected with the virus. She wanted to avoid the fate her parents had suffered.

Neve wasn't that worried about zombies. One hadn't been spotted near their compound for a long time. Even if one sneaked up on her, she could handle it. A horde of them? The droids could detect them from several miles away. That's why she built her droids. Otherwise, she could never leave the compound alone.

She brought seven anti-grav—or AG—droids in two cylinders on her back. Once she was clear of the door, Neve would press a blue button on the left strap of her backpack and the bottom of each cylinder opened. As the softball-sized droids dropped, their little AG engines took the energy from their freefall and converted it into lift, sending them whizzing through the air. Anti-grav had been a brand new technology before the virus wiped out half of the world population, but it had been too expensive for anything practical when the virus hit. Only the rich had owned hovercars or hoverbeds. Neve had scrounged for years to find seven tiny AG engines, and around them, she'd built custom-made hulls with a variety of tools.

Her friend, Zee Rampion, was the one who helped with the software, but Neve had done all of the blueprint and hardware design for each droid.

The primary function of the droids was to find zombies and live animals with motion, sound, and olfactory detection systems. They also had a small onboard laser emitter for self-defense. *Some* of their systems worked better than others.

D.O.C. was the first droid she had built, and she kept it up to date and upgraded before any of the others. D.O.C. was the only AG droid that could take a blood sample and analyze it for infection. D.O.C. used to be a bold and vivid red, but now, after so many years of work, it looked more of a reddish, muddy brick.

Her blue droid SLE-P had a battery problem. Neve tried to find a way to use the lithium-ion batteries she had gathered, but they hadn't worked out, and now SLE-P needed to recharge every thirty minutes, using up its AG engine. It would fly up about twenty feet and then drop into a freefall. The AG engine would convert that fall into power for the rest of its systems and then kick back on before it crashed onto the ground. It worked fine to keep SLE-P running, but it looked quite silly sometimes.

GRm-P was a metallic-black droid that had trouble telling zombies and living humans apart. Its olfactory sensor had broken down, and Neve didn't have the parts to replace it. To compensate, she'd programmed it to fire a two-millisecond burst from its laser, whenever GRm-P detected something with its other sensors. A live human would always cry out in pain, but a zombie would just keep staggering along, so GRm-P could use its sound detection gear to tell the difference. It was safe to say that this particular droid wasn't popular among the survivors.

The dark purple droid, DO-P was terrible at missing trees. All the droids had short-range radar to help them avoid solid objects but DO-P's was prone to malfunction. Neve had given it an extra layer of armor to compensate, but if she didn't fix the radar soon, it would take a hit one day that would do permanent damage. As a result, its armor was covered with dents, scratches and scrapes she couldn't fix right away.

Ha-P was a bright mustard yellow droid that had holes in its fuselage. When it flew in certain directions, the air would make whistling noises as the droid moved around. Sometimes, it scared off the animals, but it was pleasant to listen to, so Neve usually kept Ha-P close to her.

Her other droid SNe-Z was a coral pink, its color reminding her of the tip of her nose when she sneezed too much. SNe- Z's AG engine was prone to malfunction as well and would be replaced if Neve ever found a new one, but for now, she had to make do. The device would frequently kick the little droid around horizontally, causing it to bounce around randomly as it moved. Neve was working on a system to keep SNe-Z in place with a concentrated burst of air to counter the AG engine's push, but it was hard to calculate the exact force needed in the microseconds before the kick came. The end result was that the droid would dart around, shooting off little jets of air in every direction.

The last droid of the bunch was TRe-Z; it had once been painted blood orange and now looked more like a rusted tangerine. It didn't have a laser, but it had something much more powerful. Explosives. Its entire outer shell was covered with adhesive plates with a tiny amount of C-4 and an electric detonator. If Neve needed demolition work done, she'd send in TRe-Z to clear a path. It was dangerous though, so she never used the droid anywhere close to the compound where it could hurt someone. Since no one ever saw TRe-Z, her friends had nicknamed it Bashful.

One by one, all of her faithful droids lined up behind her and seamlessly slid back inside the canisters in her backpack. She didn't need them anymore; she'd much rather save their batteries. Neve was only a couple of miles away from The Orchard. She took her time to look at her surroundings and appreciate the lush greenery that was around the immediate area of the compound.

Her friends often wondered why she went on foot instead of taking one of their armored vehicles, but Neve didn't want to waste the fuel and resources they were fortunate to have. She'd rather save it for an actual emergency. Because of her frugal ways, their fuel and food lasted them much longer than her father had originally predicted.

She walked over a wooden bridge that had been built over a dried-up moat. Instead of water, it was filled with barbed wire, land mines, and sharpened staffs to keep zombies at bay. She reached the front gate of The Orchard and entered her code onto the keypad.

9-8-1-3

The light turned green, and the massive steel gate slid open. She stepped through the threshold and waited until the doors closed behind her. She walked down a short hallway with metal walls that hid another arsenal of weapons that Zee controlled from her tower. If there was even a hint of the virus on Neve, she would've been terminated at the push of a single button. She made her way to the second reinforced door at the end of the hallway and punched in a second set of numbers on the keypad.

1-4-0-9

The light on the keypad turned green, and the door slid open with a soft hiss. Neve breathed in the sweet smell of home. It was the crisp scent of apples and cinnamon. It was all synthetic scents and oils injected into the ventilating system just to give it a homey feel. It worked, even if it was all artificial. She removed the black backpack that held her precious droids and with great care placed them in their chargers. Neve rolled her achy shoulders a few times before she made her way to the kitchen. She set down the sack with the dead animals she'd caught that morning, knowing that Gus and Sam would prep them for dinner later that evening.

She found her best friend Bella Wright standing on a chair trying, and failing, to reach the jar of peanut butter on the top shelf. Bella grunted in frustration as she tried to balance herself on the chair and stand on the tips of her toes.

"Need a hand?" Neve mused.

Bella tucked a stray lock of her dark brown hair behind her ear and adjusted her purple, square rimmed glasses. She was, as she liked to call it, height impaired. At five feet, three inches, she hated when she had to stand on her tiptoes to reach for something. That Bella needed a chair at that moment meant that she would be on a rampage for the rest of the day.

"Why do tall people put stuff where I can't reach? Don't they know that short people live here, too?"

"You want me to yell at Gus?" Neve laughed.

"No. I'll do it. It'll make me feel better."

Neve tapped Bella on the foot. "Get down from there before you hurt yourself. I'll get it."

Bella glared at Neve playfully and pursed her lips, but carefully climbed down the chair.

Neve rolled her eyes. "Don't give me that look. It's not my fault I'm four inches taller than you."

Bella stuck out her tongue at Neve and then giggled.

Neve smirked and scanned the shelf. "Peanut butter, right?"

"Yes, please," Bella said.

"All right." Neve easily reached the jar. "Need anything else while I'm up here?" She handed Bella her prize.

"Nah, I'm good." Bella opened the jar and began to make herself a peanut butter and grape jelly sandwich. "Want one?"

"No, thanks." Neve hopped off the chair and put it back next to the dining room table.

"Are you sure? I don't mind making an extra one for you." Bella expertly spread the peanut butter on a slice of whole wheat bread.

"I don't like peanut butter," Neve confessed.

Bella's hazel eyes widened in surprise, and she studied Neve as if her friend had just sprouted a third eyeball in the middle of her forehead. "Since when?"

"Since . . . always," Neve said.

"PB and J is delicious and nutritious. There is clearly something wrong with you." Bella shook her head and turned her attention back to her sandwich.

"Tell me something I don't know," Neve said as she leaned against the kitchen counter.

Pointing to the sack on the floor, Bella nodded to Neve. "Get anything good today?"

"Two rabbits and a quail."

"Slim pickin'," Bella said.

"Better than nothing."

"True." Bella took a bite of her sandwich.

"How's Briar doing with the garden? It would be nice to get some veggies and give the animals time to breed," Neve said.

"Just some tomatoes and a few tiny strawberries. She says the soil is too dry for them to thrive the way they're supposed to."

"We're gonna have to look past the perimeter," Neve muttered as she gazed out the window.

"You know it's not safe."

"What choice do we have? We can die in here or out there." Bella sighed.

"Don't start. I don't need a sermon," Neve groaned, pinching the bridge of her nose. "We're running out of options. We should see if maybe there are other survivors. Maybe we can join forces . . . or something. Fuck if I know."

Bella shook her head. "More people to feed? More people to worry about and take care of? We're struggling enough as it is."

"I'm sorry. I just don't know what else to do," Neve whispered.

"I know, sweetie. I know."

Bella stared off into space. Her messy bun was looking more disheveled than usual. Neve noticed a few knots in Bella's brown hair that weren't there a month ago.

When was the last time she even brushed it?

Based on the way Bella gobbled up her sandwich, Neve wondered about the last time she had actually seen her eat something. She made a mental note to keep a closer eye on Bella. The last thing she wanted was to lose another friend and the only medic in the compound.

Neve didn't need to ask what Bella was thinking about. All of her thoughts were always the same.

Teddy.

Poor Teddy.

Zombie Teddy . . . Bella's fiancé.

He was currently living in one of the many rooms in the basement and being subjected to Bella's cures. Neve knew the reinforced steel doors would keep him away from everyone should he find a way to get out of his chains. Neve was still surprised that she had allowed Teddy to stay in the compound. She understood Bella's reasons though; it was hard to let go of someone you loved and who had loved you in return.

"How's it going with Teddy?" Neve ventured.

Bella always stiffened when she heard the question. Neve could see the wheels inside Bella's head turning, as if she were trying to find the best way to answer that particular question.

Bella shook her head and said, "The same. Nothing has worked. Although the good news is he won't be losing any teeth or fingers any time soon. He says a few words here and there, but he's still technically dead."

"I'm sorry," Neve whispered.

"It's not your fault." Bella took a deep breath and gave her best friend a tiny smile.

Neve needed to change the subject before Bella cried. She didn't know how to deal with a friend in tears. Because it was something she couldn't fix right away. She couldn't make Teddy human again. She couldn't fix their garden. She couldn't rid the world of the Aetervia virus. All she could do was fight. Hunt. Defend. Protect her friends as best she could. She looked down at her bare hands. They were riddled with scars, nicks, and bruises. She closed her hands and clenched them to keep herself from screaming in frustration.

Neve took a deep breath. "Any idea where Briar is?"

"In the garden trying to salvage the tomatoes that are edible for tonight's meager meal," Bella replied before licking a little bit of grape jelly from her thumb.

"Okay. I'll talk to her and see if there are any seeds I can gather next time I'm out. Something that'll grow in the garden."

"Good luck with that. She's in a pissy mood."

Neve arched an eyebrow and asked, "When is she *not* in a pissy mood?"

Bella giggled in response.

TWO

"YOU'RE ALL A BUNCH OF MOTHERFUCKING ASSHOLES. YOU KNOW THAT right?" Briar muttered as she searched through the dried-up tomatoes on the vine. She tucked her long golden blonde hair behind her ears and wiped the sweat off her forehead with the back of her hand. This wasn't what the garden was supposed to look like; all dried up like a desert. It was supposed to have rich brown soil and be filled with every single fruit and vegetable that they could possibly want.

Instead, they got dried-up twigs.

She let out a short grunt as she looked at her poor excuse of a garden. She searched through the drying vines for any good vegetables but found nothing. She just wanted to rip each plant out of the ground and throw them all in the trash can.

"We're going to die here, and it's going to be all your fault! Stupid cock-suckers. Grow dammit!" Briar shouted.

She heard the crunch of loose rocks and gravel and turned to see who was approaching. Briar smirked when she saw Neve.

"Giving the plants another pep talk I see" Neve stepped into the garden.

"I hate them. I should just set this whole fucking place on fire and start from scratch. Anything is better than this fucking bullshit." Briar pulled her gloves off and threw them on the ground.

"Yeah . . . no . . . don't do that." Neve gently patted Briar on the shoulder and tried to get her to calm down.

"I'm just tired of working hard every fucking day and not getting the results we need," Briar said.

"I know," Neve said.

"I've tried everything I can think of. But I think we need to start from scratch. Remove all of this soil or just move the garden to another part of the compound. But this is the area that gets the best amount of sunlight. So I'll have to grow them underneath synthetic light, and it won't be the same. But at least we'll have fresh vegetables and fruits."

"That's going to take a lot of work," Neve admitted.

"Well . . . it's either that or starve."

"Fine. Let me know what you need, and I'll do what I can."

"Thanks, Neve."

"No problem."

"So, how did it go today?" Briar looked to Neve.

"Two rabbits and a quail. I should have that answer tattooed on my forehead. I know everyone is going to keep asking me the same question."

Briar flinched and pursed her lips. "Yikes. What did Bella say?"

"She thinks we're screwed. I think I should go further out when I go hunting or maybe move to a different area and see if I come across other survivors."

Briar rolled her cerulean blue eyes in annoyance. Before she even opened her mouth, Neve knew what she was going to say. "Ugh. More people? More mouths to feed? Bunch of motherfucking cocksuckers—no thanks." Briar arched her eyebrow and shook her head.

Neve sighed. "It might not be as bad as you think."

"I doubt it. But you know me, always shittin' sunshine. Plus, I fucking hate people." Briar batted her eyelashes playfully at Neve.

"You don't say. I had no idea," Neve said, making sure her sarcasm was obvious.

Briar picked up the spade and dug into the soil. She broke off a piece of the root and examined it. "Dry. Fuck," she whispered. She looked at Neve out of the corner of her eye. "Anyway, what brings you here? I know this isn't a social call."

"I can't come see my friend?"

"You're so fucking full of shit, Neve." Briar chuckled. "The only reason you go out into the sunlight is to hunt, and you slather on tons of sunblock. Other than that, your pale ass hides in the shadows to avoid a sunburn. So, what's up?"

Neve shoved her hands in her pockets and sighed. "We're running out of our rationed food. The animals I'm finding aren't exactly the best. The garden isn't thriving. I need to know what kind of seeds you need me to look for. Something that will grow in this particular soil quickly before we run out of food. Something that will tide us over while we create the new garden."

"Preaching to the choir. Wanna tell me something I don't know?" Briar muttered some incoherent sentences and added, "Bring whatever you find. At this stage, there's no point in getting picky."

"All right. I'll see what I can find."

"Anything else?"

"Nope. That's all," Neve said.

"Okay." Briar knelt on the ground to finish gathering some of the tomatoes that'd had the decency to grow properly despite the fact that they hung on dry, greenish-brown vines.

Neve noticed something move in the soil. She frowned and parted her lips to give Briar a warning, but Briar spoke first. "Neve?"

"Yeah?"

"Can you hand me my knife? I left it on the table."

"Dammit, Briar. We've talked about this. Never leave your weapons where you can't reach them. Here take mine." Neve unsheathed the knife that was strapped around her thigh and handed it to Briar.

The gardener extended her tanned hand and reached for the knife. Before Briar's fingers touched the black rubber hilt of the blade, a large garden snake jumped out from underneath the dark soil and clamped its fangs on Briar's index and middle fingers. She shrieked in pain and tried to shake the vicious reptile off her hand.

With a flick of her wrist, Neve took her knife back and sliced the snake's head clean off. Her heart dropped to her stomach when she saw its ash-colored skin and red eyes. The snake was infected with the virus.

"Dammit!" Neve turned on the communicator that was always hooked around her left ear and called Bella. "I need you here now!"

"Oh God. Neve, what do I do?" Briar whimpered as she pulled the snake's head off her fingers and dropped it on the ground. There were two gaping holes filled with blood so dark it looked black.

That was the first time Neve had ever seen fear in Briar's blue eyes.

Briar grabbed Neve's arm and pulled her close so they were face to face. Her skin was covered with a thin coat of cold sweat. "Don't let me come back as a zombie. Promise me you'll kill me the moment I turn."

Neve nodded.

"Promise!" Briar cried.

"I promise."

Briar's eyes rolled back as she fainted. Neve caught her friend before she fell face down on the ground.

"Shit," Neve muttered.

Bella burst in through the back door a moment later. "What happened?"

"An infected snake bit her."

"Fuck," Bella hissed.

"Help me carry her inside."

Neve grabbed her arms and shoulders, and Bella got her legs. Together, they carried Briar into the living room.

"What's happening to her?" Neve demanded.

Bella shook her head. "I don't know. She wasn't bitten by a human. There's no way of knowing how much of the virus was in that snake. I've never had to deal with this before."

"Quarantine her?"

"Yeah," Bella replied. "All right."

They didn't have wheelchairs on this floor readily accessible to them, so they had to carry Briar themselves.

"Any idea where Gus or Sam are at?" Neve grunted.

"I haven't seen them all morning," Bella replied.

"Fuck! All right, it's just us then. Let's do this," Neve said.

"I will definitely be doing a lot of yelling later today," Bella promised.

"You and me both," Neve said.

They got into one of their service elevators and went down to the basement where all of the labs were set up. That's where her stepmother had done most of her work when she still lived in the compound with Neve's father. Now Bella was the one that had full access to all of the remaining data and equipment. Sadly, Lila hadn't left any useful information. Neve never understood why her father married Lila in the first place. Lila appeared one day out of nowhere and asked for refuge for a few days and somehow wormed her way into their lives.

Most of the computers had been wiped clean of all the research Lila had done about the Aetervia virus. Except for some scribbled notes that fell behind the desk. Whatever Lila had been trying to do with this virus . . . it wasn't a cure. Lila was trying to manipulate the virus to do what she wanted it to do. What that was . . . no one knew.

Lila had fooled everyone right from the start. But why her father? Why this compound? That was the one thing that Neve couldn't figure out.

So . . . Bella had to start from scratch.

Halfway to the laboratory, Briar twitched and convulsed. That brought Neve to attention and made her focus on the task at hand.

"Shit. We have to hurry and strap her down in case she turns," Bella said.

Once they reached the quarantine room, they set Briar down long enough for Bella to punch in the code. When the doors hissed open, Bella and Neve quickly placed Briar on the table and strapped her hands, feet, and forehead onto the hospital bed. The room was full of medical equipment, gauze, bandages, vials, and medicine to help slow the spreading of the virus. This was the room where people were either saved by amputating the infected area to keep it from spreading over the rest of the body or eventually killed when they turned. Once they turned, there was no going back, no way to bring the humanity back into the beast they'd become. Too much time had passed for them to amputate Briar's fingers. The virus was already in her bloodstream. Neve hesitated for a moment too long when the thought crossed her mind.

She looked down at Briar's unconscious body, wondering how far the virus had spread. Neve hated seeing her friend like that, but they had no choice. This was for everyone's safety. "What now?"

Bella wiped the sweat off her forehead and shook her head. "Now, we wait."

THREE

RED ROUSSEAU WAS SOUND ASLEEP IN HER BED WITH HER FAITHFUL husky/wolf mix Ajax by her side. She opened her ice blue eye and stared at the neon green numbers on her alarm clock. It was five fifty-nine in the morning. In exactly sixty seconds, her alarm would go off. Ajax lifted his head and whimpered. Her dog knew the routine by now.

Red stared at the clock and ignored her pet. She was waiting for the alarm. She would not move an inch until six on the dot. Her eyepatch was carefully draped over her clock. She wore it to cover the asterisk shaped scar on her right eye.

She counted to sixty and flinched when the alarm buzzed.

Ajax whined and walked up to the door. He gently raised his paw at her, as though asking her to take him outside.

"Morning, Ajax," she said. Ajax yawned in response.

"Oh, don't get like that. You're supposed to say 'Good morning, Red' or at least the doggie equivalent. In your case, that might be woof woof."

Red sat up, yawned, and stretched slowly. Ajax barked at her and spun around a couple of times.

"Someone's in a hurry," Red teased.

She slipped on her white tank top and picked up her eye patch. Even after ten years, she still couldn't get used to the fact that she only had one eye. She scratched the top of Ajax's head, and he gave her a sweet doggie grin in response.

"Come on, sweetie. Time to start the day," she said.

Red grabbed the shotgun that rested against the wall next to her bed. She walked out of her bedroom barefoot and still in her underwear. She didn't care. She had everything she needed as she made her way outside: her shotgun and Ajax. He sprinted toward the small patch of green grass to relieve himself.

Red and Ajax went back to her room where she brushed her teeth, used the toilet and got dressed. Together, they headed over to the kitchen. Gustavo 'Gus' Ramirez was already sitting at the table eating a bowl of instant oatmeal. He was tall and built like a tank. The white top he wore did little to cover up his muscles. His black cargo pants were always full of weapons and the bare necessities, and his dark bronze skin shone underneath the sunlight streaming in through the window. His blue-gray eyes glanced over at her as she walked in, welcoming her with a kind smile, and already her day was made.

"Hey, Red," he said.

"Morning, Gus."

Red grabbed Ajax's dog food from the top shelf and scooped out some food for him to put into his blue bowl. Her faithful dog headed straight for it and ate his meal. Then she grabbed a plastic bowl and filled it with the same instant oatmeal Gus was eating. She added a bit of milk and cinnamon, then put it in the microwave. Red leaned forward and watched her breakfast cook. One of her favorite things to do in the morning was watch the bowl spin in circles inside the microwave. It made her feel as though she wasn't the only one stuck in a never-ending carousel.

Beep! Beep! Beep!

Red pulled the hot oatmeal out of the microwave and placed the bowl on the table across from where Gus was sitting.

"You forgot your spoon," Gus said. Before she could move an inch, he got up and grabbed one from the silverware drawer and handed it to her.

"Thanks," she said.

"No worries."

Ajax continued eating, his eyes never leaving Red. She gave her pet a warm, reassuring grin to let him know she was okay before turning her attention to her breakfast and scooping up some oatmeal with her spoon. She brought the food to her lips, just inches away from her open mouth when she heard Neve's voice through the speaker in the kitchen.

"Red! Where are you?"

Red rolled her eye and took a bite despite everything. "Hey, Neve. I'm in the kitchen with Gus. What's up?" she asked between bites.

"Gus is there, too? Good. He'll be able to help you out," Neve said.

Red sighed. "Can it wait until after my breakfast?"

"I'm sorry. This can't wait. We have a serious situation right now."

Red shot Gus a worried look. Not even seven o'clock in the morning. Trouble this early in the morning could only guarantee a shitty day. "What's the situation?"

Neve told them everything that had happened to Briar in the garden.

"Dammit," Red spat.

"What do you want us to do?" Gus asked.

"I'm in the lab helping Bella stabilize Briar and doing what I can to help. I need you to go through the garden and all around the compound to see if you find any other animals or creatures that are infected. Kill and incinerate them," Neve ordered.

"Understood," Gus said.

Click.

Gus sighed. "Looks like it's gonna be one of those days."

"Yep." Red took another bite of her oatmeal.

"You coming?" Gus placed his empty bowl in the sink.

"I will when I finish my breakfast," Red said.

Gus frowned. "But Neve said . . ."

Red narrowed her eye and gave him a scathing look. She always finished her breakfast. She never knew when it would be her last meal, so she made sure she enjoyed each bite.

Gus chuckled. He knew better than to try and come between her and her food.

"I'll get our things ready and meet you in the hallway," he said.

Red nodded then calmly turned her attention back to her breakfast. A few minutes later, she emerged from the kitchen. Gus stood in the hallway, ready to get started.

"Okay. Let's do this!" Red said. Ajax barked in agreement. "Good. Let's head to the garden and see what they left for us."

Red grabbed her shotgun, and with her dog beside her, they followed Gus outside. She looked around at the garden and found it in dismal conditions. *Dried up twigs? How were they supposed to survive this year with brown leaves and dehydrated branches that gave them nothing to eat?* Red sighed and did as Neve ordered. They found the decapitated snake right away. Red knelt, picked up the reptile's head, and studied it closely.

"Be careful," Gus warned.

Ajax growled at the snake's body. She had trained her dog to sniff out and warn them against zombies. The snake was the same ashy color as a typical zombie, and the eyes were the tell-tale blood red. Red shuddered at the sight of Briar's blood staining the creature's fangs.

Gus checked out the snake's headless body. "Great. One more fucking thing to worry about," he muttered.

They tossed the snake's head and body into a metal trashcan. Gus poured some lighter fluid into the can and tossed a match inside. They stayed until the snake was nothing but a small pile of ashes. This was the only way to properly get rid of an infected body. They continued to search through the rest of the garden just to be thorough. Ajax sniffed the air and caught a whiff of something. The dog ran to the other side of the garden and barked at the corner wall where the withered watermelon patch had failed to thrive.

Red looked over her shoulder and frowned when she saw that Ajax had run off. "What did you find boy?" she whispered.

Ajax lifted his head up and whined.

Red got up and walked to her dog. Ajax had a grin on his face as though pleased that she had followed him. Then her pet turned back to the ground and dug furiously. Tiny bits of dirt and hardened soil bounced off her boots and legs. Her heart thundered against her chest as if she could somehow sense that whatever Ajax was about to unearth was bad news. She readied her shotgun and aimed it at the hole on the ground, careful to make sure Ajax wasn't in the line of fire. Sweat trickled down her temples and forehead. She closed her eyes and whimpered as though she were in pain. She could already hear the soft whispers in the back of her mind. Voices that were long gone but refused to rest in peace.

You're doomed.

Shoot!

So worthless.

Die!

Ajax continued to dig; unaware that Red was in distress. A large black rat jumped out of the ground and headed straight for Red. She screamed and fired her shotgun. Blood and body parts splattered all over her chest and the ground. Ajax whined and ran away.

Red gasped for air as she held onto her shotgun so hard her knuckles were white. She was lost in a memory. A place only she could see.

"Red!" Granny Kate said as she stood by the front door of their cottage.

"Yeah?" Red was building a moat for her castle. It was mostly made of twigs and leaves, but to her, it was as grand as the one in her book of fairy tales.

"Come inside. It's getting dark," Granny said.

"Aww. Do I have to? I'm almost finished," Red whined.

Granny chuckled and parted her lips to say something, but Red watched her grandmother's expression quickly change from amusement to horror.

"Behind you!" Granny said.

Red gasped and ran home. She didn't need to look back to know what was behind her. She already knew. Granny grabbed the shotgun that was always within reach and cocked it. Red ran as fast as her little legs could manage. Once she was out of range, Granny fired.

Red covered her ears and screamed.

Gus whispered her name softly as he approached her from behind. His hand hovered over her shoulder.

"Red, are you okay?" His hand now resting on her shoulder.

She shouted in surprise and spun around. The barrel of the shotgun was right between his eyes. One false move and he was a dead man. He glanced at Red and saw that all recognition was gone from her blue eye; in its place was a mixture of fear and anger.

Gus took a deep breath and did his best to remain calm. "Red, it's me. Gus. We're friends," he whispered.

Red had a wild look on her face. She panted as though agitated. Her face contorted in pain. "I don't know who you are," she whimpered.

"It's okay if you don't recognize me right away. I'm not here to hurt you. We're friends. Your dog Ajax seems to like me," he said.

Her husky sat down next to Gus and gave Red a friendly bark as though trying to bring her back to the present.

"Gus?" she whispered.

"Yeah, sweetie. It's me," he said.

Red lowered the shotgun and handed it to Gus as though it had burned her. "Oh God. Oh God. I'm so sorry. I can't . . . I can't control it when it happens. At least not without my meds."

"I know. It's not your fault. We ran out of your meds months ago, and it's been an adjustment. But we'll get through this," he said. Gus wrapped his arms around her. "It's okay."

"No. It's not. I could've killed you," she said.

Red pushed herself away and looked up at him, the left side of her face stained with tears.

Gus chuckled. "Yeah. That would've sucked. Lucky for me, you shot the rat instead."

Red turned around and found the rat's remains splattered against the wall and some of her clothes. She wrinkled her nose and curled her lips in disgust.

"Eww," she said.

Red crouched down next to a still intact piece of the rat's face that had its eye still attached to it.

"What color is it?" Gus asked.

"Black," she said.

"Not infected."

Red picked up the other eyeball and inspected it. "Yep. Definitely not a rat zombie." She pressed down on the eyeball a few times and grimaced playfully. "Or is it a zombie rat?"

Her smile widened as though she had just come up with a brilliant idea. "It's a RAMBIE."

Gus arched an eyebrow and gave her an incredulous look. "A what?"

"Rambie. Part rat. Part zombie," she explained.

Gus closed his eyes and massaged his temples. "How on Earth did I get stuck here with you?"

Red gave him a chaste kiss on the lips. "I'm just lucky I guess." She certainly felt that way. Lucky. Blessed. Whatever you wanted to call it, Red knew no matter what happened inside her mind, Gus would always be there for her.

Gus blushed and looked away. "Come on. We still have a lot of work to do."

"And Ajax, don't forget him."

The dog barked at the mention of its name.

Together, they all walked out of the garden determined to do a full sweep of the compound to find whatever else was lurking within their walls.

FOUR

Hunched over her keyboard, Zee typed furiously, making sure everything was up to date with all of the computers in the compound. She could access them remotely and do everything she needed to do without ever leaving her tower. Her blond braids reached her ankles and had pooled around her feet.

She adjusted her glasses and rolled her shoulders a few times. The soft blue glow of the multiple monitors fell upon her face. She had ten monitors screwed onto the wall, each showing her different parts of the compound. Zee had a visual of every single room in The Orchard and could communicate with people outside of the compound: all thanks to G.O.T.H.E.L.—Global Output Terrestrial Hub of Emergency Logistics.

It was the only place where she could give them a steady signal. It was how they communicated with the outside world while simultaneously shielding their location.

She could chat with people in different parts of the world and stay on track with the little bit of society the world offered. She took a quick break from monitoring The Orchard and checked the live feeds that were still active. With a soft click from her keyboard, she could see the Eiffel Tower in Paris. France was one of the safest places in the world at the moment. It was the one place that hadn't been ravaged by the Aetervia virus.

She let out a soft sigh and gazed at the beautiful glimmering tower. Zee knew this was an archaic way to do things but she printed the image on her screen to tape to her wall. It would join the other places she wished to visit. The Great Wall of China, Stonehenge, The Pyramids in Egypt, Chichen Itza, and so much more. She wanted to see it all. But first, they had to get rid of all the zombies and it didn't look like that would happen any time soon.

Zee took a deep breath and stretched her hands before she started working again. She was used to sleeping in two hour spurts. Everyone's safety depended on her. She was the eyes and ears of The Orchard; she saw everything from her little tower. There were cameras everywhere. Some, people knew about . . . others were ones that only Neve and Zee knew about.

The first monitor showed the front gate.

The second one showed the kitchen. Zee watched as Neve packed a plastic bowl with the stew she and Bella had cooked that evening for dinner. Her heart did a little flip as she zoomed in on her friend's face. Neve continued working on her task, chatting amiably with Bella not knowing she was being watched. Neve smiled as she placed a lid over the bowl and walked out of the kitchen.

The third monitor showed Zee the hallway near the bathroom. She caught sight of Gus and Red making out in the hallway when they were supposed to be working. Zee wasn't surprised that they were back together. Red was a thunderstorm, and Gus was a tall mountain. Steady and unyielding. He could handle Red's thunder and lightning strikes.

The fourth one was in the armory. It was important to keep track of who was taking weapons.

The fifth monitor showed her the garden. She cringed when she thought about what happened to Briar. Another reason for her to stay in her tower.

The sixth monitor was the garage.

The seventh one was the left side of the compound while the eighth monitor was on the right side.

The ninth monitor was the back of The Orchard.

And the last monitor showed her the door just outside of the tower.

Neve didn't think it was healthy for Zee to be alone day in and day out, but after a few weeks of arguing, she had stopped bringing it up. Zee assumed that she had finally come to her senses and saw things from her point of view or simply decided that Zee was too stubborn for her own good. Maybe both. Zee would never know because she sure as hell wasn't going to bring it up again. Emotions weren't exactly Neve's forte.

The communicator on her ear crackled to life. "Zee, it's Neve. I'm coming up."

"Okay." Zee leaned forward and pressed the red button on her desk that opened the first reinforced door at the bottom of the tower. Her heart hammered against her chest with excitement. And not just because she was finally getting some company. She straightened her shirt and checked her armpits for any smells that would be off-putting to Neve.

Zee closed her eyes, and for a moment, she felt Neve getting closer to her. Every step. Every footfall. Every breath and sigh as she made her way to Zee's tower. She didn't know if that connection was all in her imagination or if it was real. But she would not fight it.

Zee had put herself on lockdown on purpose. She was the only one with the code that opened the door to her little apartment on top of the tower. She had everything she needed: a room, a bed, a fully functioning bathroom, a kitchenette, books, music and more importantly . . . her computers. The table next to her desk was covered with random electronic parts and all sorts of batteries to boost the signal to see if they could reach other compounds. But they were in an extremely remote area in the Rocky Mountains. She was also setting some items aside just in case Neve needed them for one of her many droids.

Neve, Briar, and Bella took turns delivering food and supplies to Zee. They were the only ones with the codes that opened the seven reinforced doors on their way to Zee's apartment. She had canned goods and freeze-dried fruits in case of an emergency, but Neve insisted on Zee seeing a friendly face at least three times a day since she refused to leave her room.

Zee heard the loud buzz at her door. Her apartment was the only place in the entire compound that Neve didn't have access to. Only Zee could open it from the inside. Another safety precaution. It hadn't been Neve's favorite idea at the time, but when Zee explained the multiple scenarios, Neve once again backed off. The door hissed open, and Zee's heart skipped a beat. Neve was the most beautiful woman Zee had ever laid eyes on. Her throat dried at the thought of kissing those soft, full red lips. Neve's dark brown eyes crinkled as she gave Zee a warm smile.

Zee wanted to lean over and just give in to her desire, but instead she shoved her hands into her pockets to keep herself from touching Neve. She knew if she had any contact with her friend's pale skin, she wouldn't be able to stop herself from going further than a kiss.

"Hi, Zee. I brought you some leftovers." Neve handed her the small plastic container of stew.

"Thanks." Zee kept her eyes down to the floor as she took the container from Neve. Her cheeks grew warm. It only happened around Neve. Normally, Zee was the alpha female. Always. But with Neve, all she wanted to do was please her. Bow down to her every wish and need.

"It's rabbit stew," Neve said.

"Yeah. I know," Zee said.

Neve smirked. "Yeah . . . I know you know. I still have to try and make conversation with you somehow. You spend your life locked in here. You need to get some fresh air. You should come out with me. Maybe a walk around the tower? Nice and safe."

Zee would do anything for Neve . . . except that. She couldn't leave the safety of her tower. "Not really. I opened the window today. Got fresh air and everything. It was nice," Zee said.

Neve gave her a deadpan look. "That's just *weak*. You could come outside with me tomorrow . . . At least for a little while . . . I would keep you safe,"

Neve promised. She crossed her arms over her chest and leaned against the door.

"I dunno. What if someone tries to contact me? What if we have an emergency?"

"We had one today. Nothing you could've done except bear witness to our imminent demise," Neve said.

Zee gave her friend a sad smile.

Neve exhaled loudly. "They can leave a message if it's so fucking important. Dammit, Zee. I'm worried about you. It's been nine years since you set foot outside this place. You have to face the world eventually."

"You know I can't leave," she whispered.

Neve let out an exasperated sigh. "I know. Can't blame for me trying. I take it you saw what happened to Briar this morning?"

Zee nodded. She had watched in horror as her dear friend had been bitten by the snake.

"I already have Gus and Red checking the compound. But I was wondering is there any way you can do a search and keep an eye out?" Neve said.

Neve was in leader mode now. Not that she could blame her. Neve's father was dead and had left her in charge of everyone. There had been a little over one hundred survivors at the time of his death. But now? Ten the last time Zee checked, nine now that Briar was infected. She counted Ajax and Teddy as survivors, although Teddy was technically dead. Zee didn't know what to think anymore. Things were getting worse and worse every day.

"I'll see what I can do," Zee said, "but you know I'm always checking. If that snake got through, it was because it made its way underground. I have no control over that. I can only see what's on the surface."

Neve nodded and rubbed the bridge of her nose. "I know, sweetie. I know. I'm just . . . I just don't know what else to do. This is too much. This is all too fucking much."

Zee's heart melted when Neve called her 'sweetie.' If only . . . God, she couldn't believe she was doing this. Zee took a step forward and gently tucked a loose strand of hair behind Neve's perfect ear. That tiny bit of skin-on-skin contact sent a jolt throughout her entire body. Neve smiled and then frowned. Zee pulled her hand away and shoved it in her pocket.

"Anything you wanna talk about? With me?" Zee whispered.

Neve shook her head and took a deep breath. "No. I'm okay. I have to be okay. Everyone else is depending on me to not fuck everything up."

"You can stay here with me and take a moment to relax."

Neve snorted. "Yeah right."

Zee rubbed the back of her neck and bashfully suggested, "You can stay here with me and just . . . forget everything for a while."

Zee saw the look on Neve's face. She could tell that Neve was seriously considering it.

"Could I really do that?" Neve whispered.

"This is why I never leave this tower. Up here, no one can see me. No one can touch me. We are completely alone," Zee said.

"I'm so tired," Neve admitted.

"I know . . ." Zee took yet another step toward Neve and reached out to touch her hand. Zee's body quivered as she experienced the touch of Neve's skin. So warm and silky. It was intoxicating.

Neve closed her eyes and nibbled on her lower lip for a second. Zee closed the distance between them and leaned in for a kiss. Zee gasped when she felt how soft Neve's lips were.

Neve took a step back and stumbled. She grabbed a hold of the doorframe as though her life depended on it. Her eyes widened with surprise. She parted her lips as though wanting to say something, but all that came out was a soft gasp.

Zee's heart cracked a little.

"Oh God . . . I . . . I can't," Neve whispered.

"Stay," Zee begged as her voice trembled.

Neve covered her lips and shook her head. "I'm sorry." She turned around and ran out of Zee's apartment.

Once the door hissed closed behind Neve, Zee fell to the floor. She covered her mouth with her hands as the knot formed in the throat. But nothing she did could push down the sobs that racked through her body.

Stupid, stupid, stupid! How could I be so fucking stupid? Idiot. Flying too close to the sun and all you do is get burned. When will I learn? She's too good for me. Why would she ever want to be with me?

Zee covered her face and cried.

Neve ran down the hallway and pushed the elevator button several times. She rested her back against the cool wall and banged her head a few times.

What the fuck just happened?

She closed her eyes and replayed the scene she had just shared with Zee. She had been moments away from caving in. Giving herself into the moment and throwing caution to the wind. Neve couldn't erase the look on Zee's face as she walked away. Her friend looked crushed. Neve took a deep breath and said, "Fuck it."

She walked back to Zee's apartment, stood in front of the door and took a deep breath. On the other side of that reinforced steel door was the chance at true happiness. But was she willing to take that risk? From the moment Neve met Zee, she had been the truest, most loyal friend. She couldn't turn her back on her now that Zee had placed her heart in Neve's hands. She pressed her ear against the wall and her eyes teared up as she heard Zee sobbing.

Zee must've been hearing things.

Maybe sorrow leads to an unstable mind.

Perhaps getting her heart broken had made her go insane? Did someone just buzz at the door? She wiped her tears away with the back of her hand and checked the screen. It was Neve. She put her hand over the screen and shook her head. Zee couldn't look at her anymore. Whatever she thought they could've had she'd ruined by her actions. Or had she? She frowned in confusion as she punched the code into the console.

Why would she come back so quickly? Maybe she was going to tell her off? To tell her she never wanted to speak to Zee ever again. Her heart clenched at the thought. That would've been unbearable. Zee would throw herself from the top of the tower if that was what Neve had come back to do. She would rather be dead than never see her again.

The door hissed open, and once more, without fail, Zee's heart skipped a beat when she saw Neve. Her friend looked as distraught as Zee felt.

"I'm so sorry, Zee. I never . . . never meant to hurt your feelings," Neve said.

Zee opened her mouth to speak, but Neve pressed her fingers on Zee's lips. "Please. Let me finish."

She felt Neve's warm fingertips over her lips. It took every ounce of strength she possessed to stay completely still and not moan in pleasure. Even now, Neve had Zee wholly under her thrall.

Neve took a deep breath and added, "It has nothing to do with you. It's me. It's all me. I just can't afford to have any distractions. And yes, I'm exhausted from carrying the weight of taking care of everyone here and dealing with this fucking virus. But when the time comes . . . when I'm ready, trust me I will let you know. Okay?"

Zee almost whimpered when Neve pulled her hand away from her lips.

"Okay." Zee managed a tiny smile.

Neve looked at Zee adoringly, as if she had hung the moon and the stars in the sky. "You are . . . *everything*. Please understand. Promise me you won't cry anymore," Neve said.

Zee shrugged and gave her a minuscule grin. "Don't know if I can make that promise, but I'll try."

Neve took a tentative step forward and kissed Zee on the cheek.

"I'll see you tomorrow," Neve said.

"Yeah. See ya tomorrow."

Zee gently rubbed the kiss on her cheek. She felt every single part of Neve's lips still imprinted there. She was certain that Neve's kiss would haunt her for the rest of the day.

Neve winked and walked away. This time Zee didn't want to die of embarrassment. She felt the little flame in her heart grow brighter. For the first time in her life, she was hopeful for the future.

FIVE

"This is strange," Bella whispered.

She frowned as she studied Briar's chart. Bella had been checking up on Briar every day since her friend had been bitten. Briar still hadn't turned into a zombie. Which was a good thing, but confusing. A small portion of the virus was definitely coursing through her veins, but there was no change whatsoever. Briar's skin was a slate gray, not the rotting ashy color that Teddy's held. Briar would twitch once every few hours or so, but other than that she was completely still. Her chest rose and fell as though she were simply taking a nap.

"Strange," Bella muttered as she removed her glasses and rested them on top of her head. She rubbed her eyes in hopes that it would somehow make her less tired. It didn't. Bella had been practically living in the laboratory for the past week, going to her room only to take a shower, change clothes, and take short catnaps.

She took a sample of Briar's blood and put it in a small vial. Then she put it in the refrigerator to study more thoroughly later. It would keep the other seven vials company. The first few samples had given her nothing to work with, not a hint as to whether or not she was close to finding a cure for this horrific disease. Bella took a deep breath and rolled her shoulders. She had been doing nothing but typing her observations and reading charts all week.

It was time for a break.

She left Briar's examination room and went to see her fiancé. Standing in front of the door that led to Teddy's little room, she closed her eyes and pictured the way he'd been before he was bitten. Before their lives had been changed forever. It was a ritual she performed each time she prepared to enter his room.

She envisioned his golden blond hair and the way it had glinted in the sunlight. His dark chocolate brown eyes. His dimples. His blinding, perfect smile and the way he'd once laughed.

Bella took a deep, steadying breath and opened her eyes. She punched her code into the keypad and stepped into her laboratory. The room had been white, once upon a time; now there were smudges of dirt against the walls and bloody handprints to match. None of it was Bella's blood, thankfully. Sometimes she would bring Teddy lunch, whatever leftovers she could salvage from Neve's hunting trips. At least it wasn't human brains, so that was a relief. She dreaded the day they would have to feed him someone's brain. There was a table and a chair where Bella would sit and record Teddy, then study her findings. Every once in a while, she would create a serum that looked promising and test it out to see how Teddy reacted to it.

"Hi," she whispered.

Bella tried to ignore the overpowering smell of rot and decay that filled the room. No matter how many scented candles she brought into the room, the horrific smell remained.

A grunt was his only response. It was dark in the back of the room, but she knew he was chained up. The clink, clank of the chains comforted her. She was safe, for now.

Bella pushed her notes aside. She wasn't here for science. She was here to see him. She knew he was trapped in there somewhere. All she had to do was bring him back to life. For years, she had worked nonstop, exhausting every resource available to her. All she needed was the right combination of chemicals to counterbalance the mess Neve's stepmother had made. The right amount of *something* that could change everything, not just for Teddy but for everyone all around the world.

"How are you?"

"D–dead . . ." he groaned.

"You're not dead. You just need to rediscover your zest for life, that's all," Bella replied.

Teddy let out a dry, throaty chuckle.

Bella smirked. Dead or alive, she could always get him to laugh.

The chains jangled as he moved closer to the fluorescent light of the room. Her heart always leapt to her throat no matter how many times she had seen him. It always killed her to see parts of him decaying. He had spent the past three years as a zombie. He had fewer and fewer moments where he remembered who he was. Some of her *cures* kept his skin from completely rotting, and it kept his stomach from distending, which is what happened to zombies when they ate too much food they couldn't properly digest because they were technically dead.

Bella thought about how handsome he used to be. How they'd always held hands when they walked around the once lush garden. The rose he gave her when he asked her to be his girlfriend. The following year, he took her to the same garden, offered her another rose and asked her to marry him. All he had was a simple gold band to offer, but that was all she needed.

She'd said yes at least a dozen times as he'd kissed her over and over again.

Bella remembered the love, the warmth, and the joy. Now all that remained was death and decay.

But that was a lifetime ago. That was before he was bitten by Martha, the old cook. She had ventured out of the compound, past the perimeter. Teddy had been outside because he thought he'd seen something suspicious. Martha snuck up on him and bit him on the arm. Bella could still hear that roar of pain and anguish as he transformed into a zombie before her eyes. On a table just like Briar's.

She had begged Neve to let her keep him in the basement.

"No, abso-fucking-lutely not! You chop his head off or I will," Neve had said.

"Please. I can save him. I can use him to find a cure!"

"And if he escapes, he'll infect us all. What then?"

"It won't happen," Bella had promised.

"That's right because I'm gonna chop his head off before he bites anyone." Neve had pulled out her dagger and headed to the quarantine room.

Bella had used every ounce of strength to push Neve back. She'd looked ready to kick a hole through the wall. But she'd stopped to listen to what Bella had to say.

"No! Neve, I've done everything you've ever asked of me. When my parents turned and you asked me to kill them, I did it. Every order you've ever given me, I've followed without complaint. Without question or hesitation. And I'm asking you for this one thing. I need you to trust me. I can save him. I can save everyone. Please," Bella begged. Her voice quivered as tears swam in her eyes.

Neve had pinched the bridge of her nose as though that would somehow keep a migraine at bay.

"Bella, this is a monumentally bad idea. If you do this, you're on your own. I wash my hands of this."

"Understood," she'd said with a nod.

"He has to be chained up at all times. No exceptions."

"Okay."

"Very well."

That was three years ago and countless experiments later.

But he was still one hundred percent a zombie.

Bella placed a chair in front of him and tossed some food to him. Rabbit brains.

"It's not much, but it's all we have right now."

Teddy reached out and put both brains inside his mouth. A few droplets of blood oozed out of the corners of his mouth as he chewed. Bella was used to it, so she no longer gagged the way she had at first.

"So, guess what happened last week?"

Teddy grunted in response.

"Briar fell into a coma."

Teddy arched an eyebrow. It was the closest thing to a smirk as he could get. "How?"

"An infected snake bit her while she was out in her garden," she explained.

Teddy grunted once more.

"What's that supposed to mean?"

Teddy shrugged.

"Don't give me that." Bella giggled. "I've spent enough time around you to know exactly what each grunt and shrug means."

"Briar," Teddy said, "bitch."

"Ha! That's a riot. You're the one who dated her for a whole year before you wised up and dumped her ass," Bella teased.

"Fool," Teddy replied as he clumsily pointed to himself.

Bella blushed. Even dead he had the power to make her feel like the only woman in the entire planet. Tears stung her eyes. God, she missed him so much. What she wouldn't give just to hold him, to have one more kiss.

"I have to go, Teddy. I'll see you later," she whispered.

"Ughh," he groaned.

Bella knew he hated it when she left. "I know, Sweetie. But I'll be back soon. I promise."

"Love . . . you," Teddy said.

Bella grinned. "I love you, too."

She heard the chains rattling back to the corner of the room. She punched the code, and the door hissed open. It was getting harder and harder to see him. As she walked away, she prayed that Briar somehow held the key to the cure.

SIX

"Oh God, eww," Zee said after she spat out a chewy piece of rabbit meat. Out of everything she had eaten since her arrival to The Orchard, this stew was by far the worst.

It was basically boiled rabbit meat with a few pieces of carrots and celery from their meager garden. The rabbit was chewy with barely any meat in it, and someone had sprinkled a bit too much salt to make up for its lack of flavor. Safe to say this meal got an F. But beggars couldn't be choosers. At least it was clean.

That was more than some people had in a week. So she took a deep breath, ready to take another bite of her meal when she heard the alarm buzz.

"Huh?" Zee carried her bowl with her and looked at the monitor. There, in the distance, was a man. And he was headed straight toward their compound. "Shit," she hissed.

She set her bowl on the table and turned on her communicator. "Neve, are you there?"

There was momentary static and then she heard Neve's voice. "Hey, Zee. I'm here. What's going on?"

"There's a man headed our way."

"What?" she shrieked.

"Yep." Zee adjusted her glasses and tried to get a closer look by zooming in.

Yeah. Definitely a man. No curves whatsoever.

"Zombie?"

Zee shook her head even though Neve couldn't see her. "I can't tell. He's too far away. But if he's a zombie, he's the fastest one I've ever seen. He's not straying off the path or anything like that. He's zeroing in on us. I think he's running."

"Shit," Neve said.

"What do you want me to do?"

"Ready all weapons. Prepare to open fire at my command. Call Gus, Red, Will, and Sam, and tell them to wait for me at the front door when I get back just in case. I'm gonna send out my search droids so they can get a closer look at him. Until then, wait for my signal."

This was one of the reasons she loved Neve. She could go from zero to sixty at the drop of a hat. She didn't hesitate or contemplate anything when there was an emergency.

"Gotcha."

Zee sat at her desk and typed on the keyboard. Her mind was working a million miles per second, her achy fingers trying to keep up with her commands. Every camera in front of the compound was aimed at the stranger. She needed to see him from every angle imaginable so she could warn Neve should anything change. Not that he'd have a chance in hell. Neve practiced martial arts and knew how to use every blade in the compound. Even a butter knife was a deadly weapon in Neve's hands. The stranger would be headless by the time he took a step forward.

Zee had seen her in action firsthand.

At sixteen, her life had changed forever. She had lived an idyllic life in a beautiful home in the country with her mother, Nicole when the virus broke. Her golden long hair used to shimmer in the sun whenever she went outside to help her mother in the garden.

But after the outbreak?

She was trapped in the attic of her home. A prisoner in the four walls she had once treasured and adored with all her heart. All the warmth that once permeated her home was now completely gone. What Zee had wanted more than anything was to leave. But even if she managed to get outside, she had nowhere to go. No one to help her. It had always been just Zee and her mother for as long as she could remember.

Her mother had turned into a zombie. She had been working in the garden when a boy infected with the Aetervia virus snuck up on her mother and bit her on the leg. Zee stood by the kitchen window, horrified, as her mother turned into a monster. For several months, her mother did everything possible to get back inside the house.

Zee had grabbed everything she could carry and moved it up into the attic. She'd taken down the satellite dish on the roof of their house and repurposed it. Always naturally gifted with computers and any type of technology, she'd rewired the dish to the old radio in the study and connected it to her laptop. It had taken a few trials and errors, but she'd finally gotten it to work. Then she spent every day sending a distress signal to anyone within range.

After several weeks of surviving on stale crackers and water, Zee had heard someone say, "Hello? Anyone here?"

Her heart jumped. She couldn't remember the last time she had heard someone's voice.

Oh God! A person! She had thought. *An actual, living, human person.*

She let out a soft gasp when she looked out the window. Standing in her front yard was a pale brunette. Her heart did a little flip as she looked at her. She had never seen such a beautiful girl in her life. She had raven black hair and skin as white as snow. Her lips were as red as blood. She had brown eyes and a lovely heart-shaped face.

She wore brown cargo pants that looked as though they had seen better days, and a long sleeve black shirt with pieces of armor stitched onto it. She looked like a warrior ready for battle. Everything about her was perfect. At least to Zee. For a moment, she thought she had finally lost her mind and that the beautiful stranger was a hallucination.

Maybe I'm dead, and she's an angel that's come to collect my soul. At least it's a gorgeous angel.

Zee snapped out of it when she saw her decaying mother emerge from the woods, making her way toward the girl. Her mother's head twitched with every step she took. Her mother's once beautiful blonde hair had fallen out in clumps. Her clothes were in tatters. But she gnashed her teeth when she saw the beautiful stranger. Zee pounded her fists against the glass, doing her best to warn her.

"Behind you!"

Zee scrambled to her feet and unlocked the attic door. She couldn't remember the last time she had opened it to go downstairs, but there was no way she would let the beautiful stranger die on her watch. She jumped down and landed with a graceless thud on the floor. A sharp pain raced up her leg, but she ignored it. She got up and ran to the front door. Zee yanked it open with one strong pull in time to watch the stranger fight in a way she had never seen anyone do before.

It was a brutal, stunning dance. Like a razor-blade ribbon pirouetting in the wind. The girl pulled out a sharp machete. She accurately and methodically hacked and slashed at her mother as if she somehow knew exactly where she needed to cut in order to stop the zombie once and for all. The stranger took one final blow, and Zee watched as the blade sliced off her mother's head.

The decaying head rolled until it stopped at Zee's feet. There . . . between her black and white Chuck Taylors was the only family she had left. Twice dead.

"Are you okay?"

Zee's head snapped up. Her eyes locked with the stranger's brown eyes. Zee quickly nodded.

"Did you send the distress signal?"

"Yeah . . ." Zee replied.

"How did you do it? I thought all communications were down," the beautiful girl asked.

"Huh?" Zee shook her head to snap herself out of her daze. "Umm, I used my dad's old radio, connected it to my laptop to boost it, and used the satellite to bounce the signal as far as humanly possible. It's pretty easy if you know what you're doing."

"That's amazing."

Zee shrugged. "If you say so."

The girl frowned. "I have no idea what you plan to do now. I mean . . . you could come with me if you want, but I have to get my droid to run a quick blood test before I can get anywhere near you."

"Okay," Zee replied as she nudged her mother's head out of the way with her foot. It rolled off a few feet away from them. "Did you know her?" the stranger asked as she prepped her droid.

"My mother," Zee whispered.

Her eyes snapped up and locked with Zee's. "I'm so sorry. If I had known . . ."

"It's all right. It doesn't matter now," Zee said.

"Is this okay? I mean . . . my droid checking your blood? Unless you wanted to stay here . . ." She looked around at the rundown house.

"Yeah. It's all right. I don't want to stay here by myself. It's not the same with her gone," Zee replied.

"I'm Neve Blanche by the way. This is my droid D.O.C. What's your name?"

"Zee Rampion."

"Zee? That's a cute name," Neve said with a warm grin.

Zee's heart almost burst out of her chest at the sight of that smile. It was like the sun bursting through the clouds after a thunderstorm.

"It's a nickname," she whispered as she felt her cheeks grow warm. Zee rolled up her sleeve as D.O.C. slowly made its way toward her. It sprayed some antiseptic over her arm. She barely felt the pinprick as the droid expertly withdrew her blood.

Neve had a pensive look on her face while she tapped her lower lip with her index finger. "Let me guess. Zoe?"

Zee gave her a bashful grin and shook her head. "No. Not Zoe," she said.

"Ziva?"

"No."

"Zofia?"

Zee giggled and shook her head once more.

"I'm running out of names here. How about Zsa Zsa?"

"It's short for Zelda."

"Oh my God. That's adorable. I love it even more," Neve replied.

D.O.C. beeped cheerfully and flashed a green light, indicating that Zee was clear.

"All right. You're good. Ready?" Neve asked as she extended her hand out to Zee and gave her a warm smile.

Zee's hand trembled as she reached out to her. This would be the first time in months she had been touched by another human being. She had a good feeling about her. Neve's hand was rough and warm. The hand of a person who worked hard every single day. She could get used to being around someone like this.

"I have to grab my things inside," Zee whispered.

"Sure thing. I'll help you carry your stuff," Neve said.

Zee nodded and led her inside her house. She wasn't sure how she felt about not being able to live here anymore. But anything was better than being completely alone.

"She kept coming back trying . . . to eat me. She knew I was in the house somewhere," Zee said as she made her way to the attic.

"Maybe she was trying to take care of you somehow?" Neve was obviously trying to make her feel better.

Zee arched an eyebrow. "Yeah, eat my brains maybe." She let out a nervous chuckle as she climbed up the attic ladder. Zee put her laptop and a few books into her backpack.

"Is that all you're bringing?" Neve looked surprised.

"Yeah. I travel light."

Neve nodded. She stared at Zee's hair for a moment too long. Enough to make Zee touch her hair self-consciously. She hadn't been able to brush it for a while. She knew it had gotten a little matted. But a part of her liked it.

"Anyone ever tell you that your hair is really long?"

Zee blushed and looked down at the ground. Her hair was halfway down her back. "Haven't been able to cut it for a while."

"It looks nice. I think it suits you perfectly."

Zee never cut her hair after that.

SEVEN

NEVE GRABBED HER FAVORITE SAWED OFF SHOTGUN AND HER FATHER'S machete and headed out the front gate. She re-tied her armor until it was comfortable. The moment she set foot outside of the compound, she pressed the blue button on her left shoulder strap. Her seven search droids beeped to life and zipped away from her backpack, going in the direction she had coordinated beforehand. The crackle of static caused her heart to jump, but she quickly realized that it was her communicator. "You're going alone?" Zee asked. "Why aren't you waiting for Gus and the others? I already called them, and they're on their way."

Neve rolled her eyes. She should've known Zee would keep every camera on her and question every decision she made from every angle in existence.

"They're taking too long. Besides I can handle one guy," she replied.

"Dammit, Neve. You're such a bad liar. People are dropping like flies around here. Now's not the time to prove what a fucking badass you are. We already know that."

"Over and out." She turned off her communicator and kept walking.

Moments later, she heard Zee's voice once more.

"Don't you *over and out* me. You know I can override everything in this building and drag your ass back to your room if I have to," Zee said.

"You're so cute when you're angry," Neve teased.

"Don't change the subject!"

Neve giggled. She knew Zee was flustered now that Neve was actively flirting with her. "Oh my God. I can actually hear you blushing. Don't worry so much, Sweetie. I'll be okay."

Zee sighed. "Neve . . . promise me you'll be careful."

She heard the fragility in her friend's voice. Neve knew Zee would fall apart if anything happened to her.

"I promise."

Neve wasn't sure if she misheard but she could've sworn she heard Zee whisper *I love you*. She couldn't think about that right now. *Love*. That four-letter word was too dangerous. It clouded everything, just like it had with her father. He hadn't seen Lila for who she really was, a manipulative liar.

Lila cared about one thing and one thing only, her looks. Her delicate features and perfectly thin nose were all she focused on when she spied a mirror. She'd always looked at everyone in the compound as though they had rolled around in shit and mud. When she wasn't admiring her beauty in the mirror, Lila had spent endless hours mixing chemicals and oils, trying to find the cure for old age. A cure to stopping the one thing Neve now knew she feared the most, the fading of her beauty.

She wished her father had stopped Lila before things had gotten out of hand. But he was blinded by love.

Lila had knocked on their front gate one day and asked for help. Charles, drawn to her beauty and wit, had quickly fallen for her. Neve remembered watching from the sidelines, wondering why her father hadn't seen through the veil of lies.

Theirs was a whirlwind romance. They were married after only six months. The day of their nuptials had left Neve reeling. She didn't want a new mother. She didn't want her living with them in their home. Sleeping where her mother had slept. Touching the same walls her mother had touched.

But there was nothing she could do about it. Her father was happy, so she'd remained silent as she watched everything unfold.

Charles had done everything he could to protect his new wife from everyone, had given her everything she wanted. She'd played the perfect part of the pampered wife until Neve got in Lila's way. She'd seen right through her stepmother. Lila dodged questions or gave only half-truths. No one could get a straight answer out of her. Neve never trusted her and always kept a watchful eye on her. She knew Lila was envious of Charles' undeniable devotion to Neve but there had been more to it. Something darker that had kept Neve on edge, always suspicious of Lila's intentions with her father and the Orchard. But things were different now. Her father was gone and there was a new stranger in the midst. After Lila, every stranger was viewed as a threat.

D.O.C. was the first search droid to return, bringing her back to the present. It had taken a clear picture of the stranger. She let out a sigh of relief when she saw the image on the droid's screen. She used her thumb and index finger to zoom in closer to the picture. His eyes were clear, not blood red. His skin, while pale and sweaty, wasn't rotting or ashy. He wasn't a zombie. But that didn't mean they were in the clear. He could've been bitten and fighting off the infection for all she knew.

What do you want?

GRm-P and Ha-P came back with similar images except different angles. The stranger was handsome. Even she could admit that. He was blonde with sharp features and dark blue eyes. But there was something oddly familiar about him. Neve couldn't put her finger on it.

Where did she know him from?

Neve gathered her things and continued walking toward the stranger. All the while she wondered what he wanted and how had he found them. The compound was large but in a very isolated area. You had to know exactly where it was in order to find it. He was either incredibly lost or he had a secret.

When he was a few feet away, Neve fired a single round up at the sky and then aimed her shotgun at his chest. "Stop right there!" she roared.

Even from this distance, she was sure she could get a good chunk of him if she really wanted to. The stranger stopped walking and slowly lifted his hands above his head. She noticed his chapped lips and the way his chest heaved in and out. The man was clearly exhausted.

"Who are you? What do you want?"

"My name is Jack," he said between pants. "I'm looking for shelter. Maybe some food or water . . . please."

"Are you infected?"

"No." Jack shook his head. "Prove it," she said.

Jack frowned, obviously confused. "You wanna see me naked?"

Neve rolled her eyes. *Men.*

"No, smartass. One of my droids will run a quick blood test. If you fail, you die. Understood?"

Jack smirked but agreed to the blood test. Neve programmed D.O.C. and had it draw a small sample of Jack's blood. He flinched when the droid withdrew the needle and placed a bandage on him. D.O.C.'s circuits whirred to life as it analyzed the blood sample. The light flashed green. He was clear. The virus was not in his body, and he wasn't an immediate threat to her friends.

Neve lowered her weapon. "Fine. You can stay for a few days. After that, you must leave."

"Thank you." He looked visibly relieved.

She walked up to him. "Here." Neve tossed him a bright red apple. She always kept a couple of apples in her backpack. It bobbled in his hands, but he didn't drop it. Small test but it let her know he was really exhausted. A healthy person would've caught it easily on the first try. No fumble.

Jack ate the apple within moments. It was a rare treasure. Apples were one of the few things that grew on the compound without any help. He even ate the core, spitting out the seeds and saving them in his front shirt pocket. Neve frowned when she saw him do that. She wasn't sure what to make of it since it seemed harmless. Perhaps he wanted the seeds to plant somewhere else, just like she planned on doing with their garden in the compound. She would have to ask him later. When he was finished with the apple, Neve handed him a canteen of water and told him to help himself to as much as he wanted.

"Oh God. Thank you so much. You're a lifesaver." His Adam's apple bobbed up and down as he drank.

"Do you need to rest?"

He wiped his mouth with the back of his hand. He looked at the compound and thought about it for a moment.

As though reading his mind, Neve said, "Not too far. Maybe a mile or two."

"Well, I made it this far. I can go a little further."

For several minutes, they walked side by side in silence. Neve glanced at him out of the corner of her eye. She wished everyone came equipped with a handbook, that way she would know everything about them right off the bat. Life would be a lot easier if everyone was like that.

"So . . . *Jack* . . . if that's even your real name," Neve said.

"There are a lot of people named Jack," he replied.

"I'm sure there are. But Jack is actually a nickname not a proper name," Neve countered.

"Agree to disagree. Thanks again for the apple and the water."

"Not a problem." She stopped walking abruptly and placed her hands on her hips. "How did you find us?"

Jack stopped as well. "What do you mean?"

"I mean how did you know where we were?"

"I didn't I just walked," Jack replied.

She arched an eyebrow and pursed her lips.

"You walked?" Neve echoed.

He nodded.

Neve ran her fingers through her hair and did her best to suppress the urge to beat him senseless. The only thing that kept her from doing any of that was that she knew Zee was watching her, and Jack had cooperated with her until that moment. For all she knew, he was telling the truth. Or he was the greatest liar she had ever met. There was no way of knowing.

Wasn't this what she had wanted? To find other survivors? Except . . . this wasn't the way she'd wanted to go about it. She wasn't sure she liked the way *Jack* had showed up all of a sudden.

"Listen to me very carefully. If you come inside my home and try to hurt my friends, I will rip you apart. I will yank your brains out of your skull and feed them to Teddy. Do we understand each other?"

"Y-y-yes," he stammered.

"Good. Come on, we're almost there," Neve said and continued walking. She bit the inside of her cheek to keep herself from grinning. She loved the fact that she scared him, even the tiniest bit.

Neve glanced up at the tower where Zee's apartment was located. She thought about that moment they'd shared the other day.

I'm such a mess. She deserves someone better than me. Someone who can guide her toward the sunlight. Someone who knows what the hell they're doing.

She knew Zee was watching them as they approached the gate. She gave a playful wink meant for her.

"Someone over there?" Jack asked.

"No."

"Then why did you just wink?"

"How about you mind your own fucking business before I toss you head-first into this moat?" Neve said.

"Sorry. Just curious," Jack muttered.

They walked over the bridge, and he glanced down at the moat. His eyes widened in surprise when he saw all the barbed wire and sharpened staffs.

"You live here?" Jack was obviously impressed.

"Yeah. I own and run this place," Neve admitted.

Jack let out a low whistle.

"Turn around," she commanded.

Jack did as she asked. She punched her code into the keypad and the massive steel doors opened. She asked him to do the same thing when she punched in the second set of codes.

"Come in," she said.

"Yes, ma'am."

Jack walked a few steps past her and stepped inside the compound. Gus appeared as soon as Neve walked through the door.

"What the fuck, Neve? Why didn't you wait for us?" His deep, masculine voice boomed as he spoke.

Red, Will, and Sam stood behind him, mostly amused at the exchange between them.

"You were taking too long," she lied.

"I had to find out through Zee you were gone. But we'll talk about that some other time. Now, who's *this* motherfucker?" Gus turned his steely blue-gray eyes at the stranger.

"Jack," Neve said.

"Jack? No last name?" Gus arched his eyebrow.

Neve shrugged. "Don't worry. We'll find out soon enough. Gus, please show Jack to one of the guest rooms and have someone bring him some food and water."

Gus gave Jack a sideward glance. "Come on," he muttered.

"Thank you," Jack said.

Neve grabbed Jack's arm before he walked away and whispered, "Don't make me regret letting you stay here."

Jack gave her a single nod and walked away with Gus.

Red walked up to her and said, "Fresh meat. I'm surprised you let him live."

"Me too. But it didn't feel right to let him die out there," Neve admitted. "Especially since he was cleared by D.O.C."

Red ran her fingers through her short crimson hair. "Want me to keep an eye on him?"

"Yeah. As long as it's your good one," Neve teased.

"Ha, ha, ha," Red said in a dry tone.

Neve chuckled and shook her head. "Never gets old."

"Red is right. This is the first time in a long time we've had someone in the compound," Will said. He was a short Mexican man with black hair and brown eyes who always looked like he was ready to break into a smile. He was a good person to have around when you were sad. It was like having sunshine in human form.

"You think I don't know that?" Neve said, "Trust me, Zee and I will go through all of the proper background checks. I already have a sample of his blood."

"Want me to take it up to her?" Sam asked.

He was a tall blonde that lived in tank tops and cargo shorts even in the middle of winter. He was one of the most dependable people in the compound.

But Neve wanted to visit Zee, and she needed a valid excuse to keep going up to see her.

She shook her head. "No. I got it, thanks. I just want you to keep a close eye on Jack. We'll see how he does here in the compound. If he seems trustworthy, he can stay. If not, then we'll give him water, food, and send him on his way."

"Ouch. Harsh," Red said.

"I would rather die out there than be killed by Neve. Seriously," Will said.

"Good to know," she replied.

"All right. We've got our marchin' orders," Red said.

"Come on," Sam said.

The three of them left Neve alone with her thoughts. Her gaze went to Zee's tower. She couldn't stop thinking about Zee's eyes. They were a blue so deep she wanted to stare into them until she felt like she would drown in them.

What would happen if she gave in? For just one moment?

I wonder . . .

Neve's palms were damp as she made her way upstairs to Zee's apartment. This had never happened in the nine years that Zee had been living in The Orchard with them. Neve was never nervous or uncertain when she went to visit her.

Now, she was both.

She took a deep breath and steadied herself as she pushed the buzzer and waited. Her heart skipped a beat when Zee opened the steel door with an impish grin on her face.

Then she noticed things about her friend that she hadn't before. Her cheeks were pink, almost as if she had been blushing moments before Neve arrived. Her blonde braids touched the floor and dragged at least a foot behind her. Zee had on a pair of baggy jeans, a white tank top, and a red plaid shirt with the sleeves rolled up.

Zee shoved her hands into her pockets. "So? Who's the new guy? He's kinda cute."

"Most people start with hello," Neve said.

"I'm not most people," Zee replied.

"I know."

"Who is he? You know my cameras don't go out that far, and I can't hear anything. What did he say to you?"

Neve sat down and told her everything that had happened.

At least the parts Zee didn't already know.

Zee flopped onto her desk chair and frowned. "That's it? He didn't say where he's from? Where he's going? What he's running away from?"

Neve shook her head.

"We should have Bella interrogate him," Zee said.

Neve crossed her arms over her chest. "Why Bella?"

"He might wanna talk to someone who's actually . . . you know . . . nice," Zee replied and then winced as though waiting for the backlash.

Neve's eyes widened in surprise. "And I'm not nice?"

Zee's face softened, and she gave Neve a warm grin. "You're great with your friends. But you'd sooner chop off his nuts than smile. Sometimes, you're downright terrifying."

Neve chuckled in response. She didn't mind that one bit. It was a mantle she'd had to take on at a young age to get people to listen and take her commands seriously. She needed to be stronger and tougher than everyone . . . even the men. Especially the men.

She reached inside her pocket and pulled out a small vial of blood. It was leftovers from the sample D.O.C. took from Jack. "Think you can do a search on him based on this sample of blood?"

Zee took the vial from Neve's hand and studied it.

"I can try. I'll let you know if anything pops up. What do you wanna know?"

"Parents' names. Blood type. Social security number. Shoe size. Height. Weight. How many teeth he has in his mouth. Everything. Every single thing you can find," Neve said.

Zee rolled her eyes and smirked. "I should know better than to ask. Of course you want everything."

"Don't we all?" Neve mused.

Zee shrugged. "I dunno. The only thing I really want is to finally see what's left of the world. But I don't see that happening any time soon."

"If Bella finds a cure? Who knows?"

"Yeah," Zee whispered.

"Umm. Anyway, do you need anything else besides that?" Neve motioned at the blood sample.

Zee shook her head. "Nah. I already have everything I need right here."

Neve wanted to flirt back. Say something funny or witty, but instead, she clammed up and remained silent.

Zee must've noticed because she gave her a warm smile and said, "I'll get this back to you as soon as possible."

"Good. Ummm. Thanks," Neve stammered. She rubbed her damp hands on her pants and made her way toward the door.

"You're welcome," Zee said.

"All right . . . I'll see you later."

"You know where I'll be."

Neve nodded and walked out of Zee's apartment without another word. She didn't realize she was holding her breath until the door hissed closed behind her. Neve inhaled deeply and pressed her forehead against the cold metal door.

Coward. I'm such a fucking coward.

She closed her eyes and pulled herself away. She would try again another day.

EIGHT

BELLA ADJUSTED HER GLASSES AND TOOK A DEEP BREATH. SHE HAD a warm tray of mashed potatoes, green beans, and a small meat patty from their frozen rations for their new guest. She already had her orders from Neve. She had to get as much information out of him as possible. Bella didn't understand why everyone was making such a big fuss over it. Just a new guy in the compound. They'd had people stumble onto The Orchard before. The last person to find them was Will, and that was eight years ago.

Wait. That can't be right.

She did the math in her head. Will had been sixteen years old when he pounded his fist on their door shouting, *"Ayúdeme, por favor!"* over and over again. Barely able to speak any English, but they didn't need words to see a starving kid in trouble. With patience and Zee's translator program, they figured everything out. He was lost, scared, and hungry. That was the only time Bella had ever seen Will sad. After that, he was all smiles and cheerful.

Neve had always been cautious, especially around new people. She always had to be on the alert when everyone's safety rested on her shoulders. Bella knocked on the door and waited.

"Come in," Jack said.

The door slid open, and Bella had to catch her breath. Jack was handsome.

A little thin, and he had dark circles underneath his eyes, as if he hadn't had a decent night's sleep in a long time. But more than that, he looked haunted. As though he had spent several years of his life witnessing untold horrors. *Why didn't anyone tell me he was so cute? Or maybe I've gotten to the point that anyone with an actual pulse looks good to me.*

"Jack . . . right?" Bella said.

"Yeah, and you are?"

"Bella Wright." She placed his meal on the small table next to the door and extended her hand.

He took her hand and shook it gently as if she were some delicate creature that would break somehow.

"Last name?" Bella smiled.

"Smith," he replied.

Bella cocked an eyebrow. "Seriously?"

He met her steady gaze and said, "Seriously."

"So, what brings you to our neck of the woods?"

"Just trying to stay alive." Jack reached for the tray and sat on the corner of the bed. "You don't mind, do you? I'm starving."

Bella took a step back. "Yeah, of course. Do you want me to leave?"

Jack looked her up and down a few times and then adverted his eyes when he realized what he was doing. Bella's pulse quickened. He was checking her out. It had been a while since anyone had given her the once over like that. She felt her cheeks grow warm.

"Sorry, it's been a while since I've seen another person. Let alone a beautiful woman." Jack blushed.

Bella self-consciously touched her messy hair and gave him an awkward smile. "I'll take that as a compliment."

Bella turned around to leave when she heard him say, "You can stay . . . if you want."

She looked over her shoulder. "Are you sure?"

Bella was genuinely pleased that Jack had asked her to sit with him. The thought of spending time with someone new gave her a jolt of excitement she hadn't felt in a long time. She had butterflies in her stomach. It was a welcome change of pace from the constant worrying she did every day.

"I promise not to stare at you," Jack replied. He picked up the fork and ate.

"Okay." Bella sat on the chair next to his small desk, and they were silent for a few minutes while he ate his meal.

"Sorry if the meat is a little dry," she said, "but I figured you'd want an actual meal and not have to deal with stringy stew."

Jack swallowed. "Are you kidding? This is a five-star meal compared to what I've been eating lately, which isn't much. Some wild berries if I was lucky. But mostly sunflower seeds I collected from a field I passed along the way."

"How is it out there?" Bella couldn't remember the last time she'd set foot outside of the compound. All her time was spent taking care of her friends, trying to find a cure for the virus and monitoring Teddy's progress.

Jack shuddered involuntarily. "You don't wanna know."

Bella tucked a loose strand of hair behind her ear. "I kinda do. I was practically raised here. I mean, I remember a couple of things about what life was like before the virus. But nothing major. Mostly my backyard because I loved being outside and a swing set."

Jack took another large helping of his food. It was as if he was using it to buy himself time before answering her question. "I know what you mean, and I wish I could tell you that there's something else out there that's better than your life here. But I'm not a very good liar."

"Seriously?"

"Don't believe me?" Jack gave her a playfully challenging look. "Go ahead. Ask me anything."

"How about this? Tell me three things about yourself and make one of them a lie."

He took a deep breath, as though bracing himself for the onslaught. "All right. I was born in Arkansas, I'm six feet tall, and I was raised by a crazy little old lady who loved playing cards."

He blushed halfway through the statement. Bella giggled. "You're not six feet tall."

"Yeah. Hard to lie about my height. I'm actually five-ten."

"Two inches make a difference?"

"Trust me. It makes all the difference." Jack gave her a mischievous wink.

Bella smiled and giggled. Again, this handsome stranger had caught her by surprise. She could laugh around him so easily. But it made her feel as though she were betraying Teddy somehow. In the back of her mind, she pictured her fiancé before he was bitten. The whole world could've been blown to oblivion, and as long as she had Teddy by her side, she would've been all right. Without him, she felt unhinged, a ship drifting in a pitch-black sea.

A lump formed in her throat as that thought crossed her mind. She felt like that every single moment of every day. There had to be more to life than that. There had to be more than just survival. Otherwise, what was the point? "I should get going, I have a lot of work to catch up on."

"Okay. I guess I'll see you around then. Thanks again for the food."

"Not a problem," she said. Bella stood and adjusted her glasses.

"Oh, before you go. Can I ask you a question?"

"Yeah, sure," Bella said.

"What's the deal with Neve? Has she always been so . . . you know . . . intense?"

Jack grabbed his glass of water and drank a few gulps of it. She couldn't help but compare him to Teddy. The only thing her fiancé drank was blood that dripped from the brains she fed him every once in a while.

"I've known her my whole life. We grew up here. She was always a serious and precocious child. But it got much worse when her father died."

"What happened?"

Bella then remembered that she was supposed to get information on him.

"I'll answer your question if you tell me something about yourself."

Jack sighed.

"I knew there was a catch," he muttered.

Bella smirked. "There always is."

Jack ran his fingers through his blond hair and took a deep breath. "I was at a compound similar to this one. A little smaller, and it looked more like a massive gray Lego block than a castle. Not as much food" —he motioned to his plate— "but we managed. Then the zombies started attacking. First in small groups. We defended ourselves easily. But then it got much worse. The groups were bigger and bigger. I kept telling everyone we should grab our shit and move. No one wanted to take the risk. They all thought we would be safer indoors."

"What happened?"

Jack shook his head. "Your turn."

"Neve killed her father when he got infected and became a zombie. She was fifteen."

"Whoa."

"Yeah. Which explains her issues with almost everyone and everything."

"What do you do here?"

"I do research," she said.

"Research on what?"

"Zombies."

Jack leaned forward as though intrigued. "Oh yeah? What have you discovered?"

"Lots and lots of things." Bella had no intention of telling him what she'd learned. Even though she was feeling comfortable around Jack, she still didn't want to divulge too much information.

"I bet."

"What happened to your friends?" Bella met his eyes.

Jack took a deep breath, and for a moment, he had a far off look on his face, as if somewhere in his mind he was reliving that moment all over again. "My girlfriend, Mary was pregnant. So, we packed up our stuff and left. That night, there was a security breach on the compound, and the zombies attacked. We could still hear their screams as we escaped. But we kept on going."

He ran his hands over his face. Tears swam in his eyes, and he swiped them away angrily.

"I'm so sorry," Bella said.

"Don't be. I made my choice and so did they."

"What happened to Mary? Why isn't she with you?"

Jack took in a sharp intake of breath as if someone had just punched him in the stomach. "We walked for weeks. Spending time inside abandoned houses, killing the odd zombie here and there, but we didn't find another compound. Then Mary's water broke. She wasn't due for another month. It . . . there were complications," he said. He lowered his head as though praying. "They didn't make it," he whispered.

Bella covered her lips. She didn't know what to say. All she had were questions. She was a natural problem solver. A doctor. A scientist. All she wanted to do was think and solve everything like a puzzle.

How dilated was she? Did the baby need help being turned? Maybe the baby had the umbilical cord wrapped around his neck. Did she lose too much blood?

She asked herself a dozen questions but didn't dare utter any of them out loud. She didn't want to make things harder for Jack. She hoped that he was telling her the truth and not just spinning some tale to gain her sympathy. Suddenly, Bella wasn't sure what to believe.

Maybe this is why Neve sent me to talk to him.

"I buried her with the baby still inside her. I found . . ." Jack took a shaky breath and found his composure. "I found a field of sunflowers, and I buried her there. Somewhere pretty and cheerful." He wiped a tear that escaped his eyes.

"That's terrible. I'm so sorry you had to go through that."

He suddenly got a panicked look on his face. He grabbed her hand and held it tight. Bella gasped and tried to pull it back, but he was far too strong. "You have to warn your friend. They're coming. I don't know when, but it's getting worse. So much worse than you can possibly imagine."

"How so?" Bella asked.

"It's like there are more people becoming infected every day. Almost as if there's someone out there infecting people on purpose. I can't understand what's going on."

Bella kept her thoughts of a possible cure to herself. The less people knew the better. The last thing she wanted to do was spread a false sense of hope. She pulled her hand away, and this time he let her go.

"Whatever it is . . . it'll be okay. You're safe here. You need to get some rest. We can talk some more tomorrow."

Jack's shoulders sagged a little and he let out a long sigh. "You don't believe me."

"I do. But we need to talk more when you've had time to eat and rest for a bit. I'll come back later with more water, food, and clean clothes for you, okay?"

He gave her a sad nod. "Thank you."

"You're welcome," Bella said and walked out of his room.

She took a few steps down the hall. A wave of sorrow washed over her. She didn't really understand why she was so sad for a stranger she'd just met. All Bella knew was that she felt his grief as if it were a living breathing entity. Or perhaps the weight of everything she had gone through over the past few years had finally caught up to her.

She made her way to her room. Determined to take a moment and sleep before she collapsed on the floor in the middle of the hallway. She hadn't had a decent night's sleep in ages, and the exhaustion was finally taking its toll on her.

She flopped onto her small, twin-size bed and closed her eyes. She thought about Jack and his sad, haunted eyes before she finally drifted off to sleep.

NINE

Neve turned off the monitor. She'd seen and heard every single thing Jack had told Bella. He'd sounded sincere enough. She thought he was a coward for abandoning his friends at his compound, but if there really was a pregnant girlfriend, she understood why he'd wanted to keep her safe. Neve would let him stay for a few days, after that she would have to see how useful he was around The Orchard. Everyone had to pitch in. No one got to stay for free. Maybe he could tend to the garden? Neve sighed and glanced at the calendar on the wall. What were the odds that this stranger would appear on the anniversary of her father's death?

June 7, 2113.

There had to be more to this. Things don't just happen at random.

Time to go see Daddy.

Normally she would've gone first thing in the morning, but with everything happening, she had a late start. Neve gathered her things and went out into the cemetery in the back of the compound. His body had to be cremated because of the infection, but his ashes were buried underground. There was a small silver headstone that read:

Here lies Charles Blanche.
Loving husband and father.
June 1, 2063 – June 7, 2106

Neve knelt and carefully brushed off some of the dirt and dead leaves on his headstone. She closed her eyes and imagined her father standing next to her. It's what she did whenever she felt the need to talk to him. Especially when she thought her life was falling apart.

"Hi, Daddy." Neve felt the sad smile cross her face. "I'm so sorry," she whispered. No matter how often she visited, she always started her *imaginary* conversations with him the same way.

"It's okay, Cupcake. You know I forgive you," her father said.

"I know . . . I know. I still miss you. I have no idea what I'm doing."

"You've done just fine." She pictured his kind eyes crinkling as he smiled at her.

Neve sighed. "There were a little over a hundred people living here when you were in charge. After you died, half of them picked up their shit and left without a single word. And then after a while, more people moved to other compounds where the person in charge wasn't a fifteen-year-old girl. Thanks a lot, puberty. And then more people just died or became infected with the virus. We are down to ten people in the compound, and that's counting Briar . . . who's now in a coma."

"None of what happened is your fault." At least that's what Neve imagined him saying.

"I feel like I'm a bad person," Neve said.

"Just because you can't stop terrible things from happening, doesn't mean you're a bad person. It just means that you have no control over anything, and that's scary. It's okay to be afraid sometimes."

Neve sighed. "What am I gonna do?"

Charles smiled. He leaned forward and in a mock whisper said, "You wanna know a secret?"

"Yes."

"I had no idea what I was doing either."

"You are such a liar." Neve chuckled. "I went through all your stuff in your room. You had a plan for everything except my menstrual cycle."

"That's because that was your personal private business."

She sighed as she caressed the cold headstone. "I miss you."

"I miss you, too, Cupcake. But it's time for you to go back to the real world and figure stuff out. People are counting on you."

Neve took a deep breath and opened her eyes. Her father's voice was gone, and all that remained was his headstone.

NEVE HAD A RESTLESS SLEEP THAT NIGHT. SHE WOKE UP GROGGY and covered in cold sweat. She had a desperate need for something hot and caffeinated. Her alarm blared at her moments later letting her know it was five o'clock in the morning. As tired as she was . . . duty called. She turned off her alarm and got ready to face the day.

She planned on going a little further past the perimeter in hopes of finding larger game. She took a moment and reprogrammed her droids, adding new coordinates as well as additional commands . . . just in case. Her stomach flipped once she pushed ENTER. Something told her this wasn't such a good idea, but she thought it might be her nerves doing the talking. Especially since this would be her first time venturing out on her own past the familiarity and safety of *her* woods.

Neve shook the negative thoughts out of her head and contacted Zee on her communicator.

"Hey, Zee. I'm headin' out," Neve said.

"Good morning, Sunshine. Should I contact Gus and let him know? Or should I wait until you're gone so he can pace back and forth by the front door 'til you get back?"

Neve chuckled. "I'm going alone."

"So . . . business as usual?"

"Yeah."

"Got everything you need?" Zee whispered.

Neve added a few extra knives and shuriken to the straps of her boots, then took a moment to readjust her body armor. "Yeah. I'm good."

"Be careful."

"I'll see you in a few hours. Don't worry so much."

"Okay."

Neve then heard Zee's tiny voice . . . a decibel below a whisper. It sounded a lot like *I love you.* That was the second time she'd heard that—was she losing her mind? Was she imagining things? Did Zee really say those words? She wanted to ask her more questions. But she knew if she opened that Pandora's Box, she might not be able to close it again.

I'll deal with that later.

Neve strapped her backpack over her shoulders and stepped out of the safety of her home. She pressed the blue button on her shoulder strap and released her droids from their case. She watched as they dutifully zipped away from her and scanned the area.

She lifted her face toward the sky and let the warm sunlight caress her skin. She had the usual bit of sunscreen, but still . . . she liked feeling the sunshine. It made her feel hopeful and alive. She gazed upon the bright blue sky and wondered about life before the virus, before she was born . . . if things were simpler back then. Then she looked at the scenery before her.

The sparse woods, patches of brown and green. Neve sighed and forged ahead. She hoped to find something. What it was, she wasn't sure.

Slowly, the scenery changed. Gradual enough that it took Neve a while to notice. And when she did, her eyes widened in surprise. This part of the woods was lush and full of life. There were trees here that she hadn't seen in a long time and some she had never seen before altogether.

"Wow," she whispered.

She let herself smile just for a moment. Perhaps she had been right. The only way to make sure this was the right move was to actually catch something worthwhile. Something she could take back to the others.

She explored the forest for a long time. She foraged for berries and even found some edible flowers that she'd read about in a book once. She placed everything in her bag as carefully as possible. Then she heard the soft crunch of leaves.

Neve held her breath and stopped moving for a second, hoping to pinpoint the exact location of the sound.

She looked to her left and whispered, "Oh my God."

She was several feet away from a large deer. Neve had never seen anything so powerful and graceful before. It had long lashes and dark brown eyes that looked right into her soul. Its golden-brown fur shone in the morning sun. Its antlers were almost as tall as it was. She felt bad that she'd have to kill it.

Neve ambled as she pulled out a shuriken from her left boot and threw it at the deer with the precision of a surgeon. It landed right on the deer's neck on a vein. A large spurt of blood gushed out of its wound. The deer whined and reared its front legs up in the air. It tried to run away, but it buckled forward and landed on the ground with a heavy thud.

"I'm so sorry," she whispered.

Neve pulled her knife out and plunged it into its chest, right where its heart was supposed to be. She held it there until she was sure it was dead, then pulled her knife out, wiped it on the grass, and slipped it back into its sheath. She heard one of her droids chirp at her, but it was too far off, so she didn't pay much attention to it. She checked the screen on her smartwatch to see if it was warning her about something but the image was blurry. She frowned as she tapped the screen a few times to zoom in, but the image remained out of focus.

She called her droids back so they could help her carry the deer carcass back to the compound. She pulled zip ties and a plastic tarp from her backpack. First, she tied the deer's legs together, then she covered it with the plastic tarp. Once that task was done, there was nothing left to do but wait for the droids to return.

"Unnnggghh." A loud moan came from somewhere in the woods.

Neve turned around in time to see a male zombie emerge from behind the trees. Its decomposed body was slowly but steadily making its way toward her. The zombie's left eyeball dangled out of its socket and swayed from side to side.

"What the hell?" Neve muttered. She pulled out her machete and kicked the zombie in the chest, causing it to fall on its back. The zombie gnashed its yellowed teeth and reached out to grab Neve, but she was able to avoid its grip. She kicked it on the neck with her steel-toed boot then swung her machete with one smooth arc, slicing off its head.

Before she could breathe a sigh of relief, two more zombies appeared. Neve pulled out her dagger and fought them off.

"Where the fuck did you come from?" she grunted.

Neve flinched and pulled herself away just as one of them missed biting her arm by mere inches. She screamed in surprise but escaped its rotting yellowed teeth. Neve had always thought if she ever came close to death her life would flash before her eyes, but she was wrong. She saw her parents, Bella, Briar, Gus, Red, and more importantly . . . Zee. Neve saw her friend's sweet face, her bright blue eyes that even a pair of glasses couldn't mask, her smile and her long, blond braids. She wanted to make it back to her alive, more than anything in the world. Neve promised herself that she would do everything possible to make up for her past mistake.

Neve did a backward flip, and with a roundhouse kick knocked the second zombie's head off. The third zombie was a large woman. Tall and wide, as if she had been a wrestler in another life. She lunged at Neve and fell, losing her balance on the uneven terrain of the forest. Neve cocked her shotgun and shot the zombie in the back of its neck. Blue-black blood oozed out of its wound as it fell to the ground with a heavy thud. Finally and completely dead.

When all of the zombies were dead, her droids finally returned.

"Where the fuck were you?" Neve cried.

All seven droids let out low hums and dipped closer to the ground as though ashamed that they had failed her.

She checked them and quickly realized that she had forgotten to push the warning button. Or had she? Had someone out there tampered with her droids remotely?

Fuck.

She would have Zee run a diagnostic on them.

Her heart thumped nervously against her chest as she checked her surroundings. Was there someone here? Watching her? She wasn't going to stick around long enough to find out. She was alone and vulnerable. Even if she sent a message out to Zee, it would be a long time before someone made it to her exact location. She was supposed to get the bodies together and burn them to deter other zombies from gathering. But she would have to wait until tomorrow. She felt the need to leave the forest as quickly as possible.

She grabbed the dead deer, tied it to GRm-P and DO-P. Together, they all made their way home.

Sweat was dripping down her face and back when she finally returned home. Her legs and lungs ached and burned from the exertion. She regretted not taking the truck but as always . . . she had wanted to save the fuel for an actual emergency or the off chance they found an old vehicle that required gasoline.

Neve spent the entire time going over the events that had occurred that day. She had gone almost a year without seeing a zombie, and now there had been three in a single afternoon.

She couldn't explain it. Unless . . .

Lila.

She was out there somewhere, testing Neve, testing the security of The Orchard's surroundings. Trying to get back in. But why? That's what Neve couldn't figure out. Was there something Lila had left behind that offered her the answer to her lifetime quest for everlasting beauty? They'd searched high and low for an answer as to why Lila had disappeared the night her father was mysteriously turned into a zombie. The night Neve was forced to kill him. Neve had always been suspicious that Lila had been the reason for his sudden transformation. There was no way one could have breached the compound on its own.

Unless Lila had somehow injected the virus directly into her father while he slept. With all the research she had done, she could've easily gotten ahold of something. Nothing they'd found after she'd fled provided any support for Neve's theory, but she knew in her heart that Lila was to blame.

But why zombies today . . . and how? No one controlled the hordes of creatures that roamed their lands. Had she somehow found a way? Was she testing her serums again? Was she testing it on zombies? Transforming them into a new breed of monster? The thought was almost too unbelievable to contemplate.

Then again, this was Lila she was talking about and nothing about Lila came as a surprise to Neve anymore.

She sighed and wiped the sweat from her forehead. She would have to talk with Bella about her theory. Right now, however, she needed to deal with the dead deer that was currently decomposing in the hallway. She told GRm-P and DO-P to take it downstairs to a large, walk-in refrigerator in the basement. She'd ask Gus and Sam to skin and cut the deer meat for easier storage.

She turned on her communicator. "Gus. You there?"

Seconds later, his deep, baritone voice came through. "Yeah, I'm here. What do you need?"

"Can you and Sam take care of the deer I just caught? The droids are taking it to the basement as we speak."

"No problem."

"Thank you," she said. Neve turned her communicator off and put the other five droids back in their chargers. She went to the kitchen for a glass of water. Just as she sat down to drink it, Red walked in.

"Hey, Neve," she said.

"How are you?" Neve took a sip of her water.

Red shrugged and sat down on the chair across from her.

Must not be having a good day, Neve guessed.

Red was many things: Loyal. Brilliant. Funny. But she was also mentally unstable and suffered from post-traumatic stress disorder.

She had suffered severe trauma at the tender age of twelve. She was the sole survivor of a zombie attack. She'd lost her grandmother, family and friends in her village and her eye that day. The gun they had hadn't been properly cleaned in ages, and when Red used it to defend herself, it backfired, causing her to lose her eye. Thankfully, Red had always been quick on her feet, and even with that agonizing pain, she grabbed a knife and killed the zombie that had forced its way inside her home.

For a while, Red had managed her symptoms with the medication they had on hand. But now . . . now they were out, and Red rationed her meds to use on really bad days. She was supposed to take them daily, but no matter what Neve or Bella said, they hadn't been able to change her mind. Red's symptoms were getting worse every day. Neve was at a loss. She had no idea what to do.

"You all right?"

"Something weird happened in the forest," Neve said.

"What happened?"

"I was attacked by three zombies while I was busy covering up the deer I killed. That's never happened before."

"What?"

"Yeah. It's fucked up. And you're going to hate me for this . . . but I forgot to burn the bodies," Neve said.

"WHAT?" Red roared.

"I know," Neve said and then groaned.

"You *forgot*? You?" Red shrieked.

"I panicked. I was in a hurry to leave. I was scared that there was someone watching me. I think someone tampered with my droids," Neve said.

"You know zombies are attracted to the scent of dead zombies. They have an incredible sense of smell."

"You think I don't know that?" Neve sighed and shook her head in dismay. "I'm gonna go back and burn the bodies."

"What about the zombies? What do we do if there are more out there?"

"We need to ramp up security and surveillance. From now on, there will be at least three people awake at all times. No one leaves the compound alone anymore."

"Including you?" Red cocked an eyebrow.

Neve pursed her lips and sighed. "Including me."

"You mean it?"

She crossed her arms over her chest and sulked for a moment. "I do."

"Good. We'll go out tomorrow and scout the area. See if there are any more zombies running around trying to get inside then we'll burn the ones you left behind."

"Sounds like something I would say," Neve replied.

"Which is why I'm your second in command. Or third . . . I can never be sure. I know I'm tied with Gus."

"All right. Get out of here, you smart ass. I'll see you in the morning." She gave Red a playful shove and watched as she walked down the hallway.

Things were definitely changing. Maybe Jack was right. Maybe things were just getting worse every day, and it was time to prepare for the end.

TEN

ZEE LOOKED AT HER MONITORS AND WATCHED AS NEVE MADE HER way up the tower. She nibbled on her lower lip. It wasn't dinner time, and there wasn't an emergency, at least nothing she was aware of.

Is she coming to see me? Just . . . because?

"Oh God," she whispered.

Zee scrambled out of her seat. Her long hair trailed behind her as she dashed to the bathroom. One of her braids got stuck on one of the legs of the chair. A sharp pain reached her skull, and she shrieked in protest.

"Ouch! That hurt. God damn it," she hissed as she rubbed a sore spot in her head. She tied her hair up as best as she could and made it look nice. But that was a difficult task since it was at least seven feet long.

Maybe it's time for a haircut.

She brushed her teeth, then stood by the front door and waited with bated breath.

After what felt like an eternity, the door buzzed. Zee jumped at the sound even though she was expecting it. Her heart sped up for a moment. She even had butterflies in her stomach. Zee let out a nervous chuckle; it was like being a teenager all over again. Because it was a hard habit to break, she looked at her screen and smiled when she saw Neve's profile.

God . . . please don't let her break my heart.

Zee closed her eyes and took a deep steadying breath. When she opened her eyes, she punched the code into the keypad, and the door hissed as it slid open.

Her eyes locked in with Neve's dark brown orbs, and then she quickly looked away.

"Hi," Zee said.

"Hi," Neve said.

Zee breathed in the smell of fresh soap. Neve's black hair was still damp from her shower. Small droplets fell from the end of her hair onto her white tank top and the floor. Zee clenched her fists to keep them from reaching out to Neve.

"I'm still working on getting information on Jack if that's what you wanna talk about. Someone worked really hard to keep his records confidential," Zee said.

"Oh . . . yeah," Neve said. "As soon as you have anything, let me know. Also . . . can you run a diagnostic on my droids? Something weird happened to them today, and I wanna make sure it was me that forgot to push the warning button and not someone hacking into them remotely."

"Yeah. Not a problem. I can do that ASAP." Zee gave an affirmative nod. She frowned and waited for Neve to say something else. This was definitely something she could've said to her over the communicator.

Neve stood there as though lost.

"Are you okay?" Zee asked.

"I was lonely." Neve shoved her hands into her pockets and shrugged, as if admitting that was the worst possible thing she could do. "God . . . that sounds fucking pathetic, doesn't it?"

"How can you be lonely? You spend all day bossing people around. It's your favorite thing to do," Zee teased.

"Yeah, not really the same thing," Neve replied.

"I bet . . ." Zee said.

"So . . ."

"Do you wanna come in?"

Neve nodded and stepped into Zee's apartment.

"I, umm, found this in the kitchen. It's kinda old, but I thought, what the hell. You know?" Neve then pulled a bottle of wine out of her bag.

"Oooh," Zee said.

"We were saving it for a special occasion, but we haven't had one of those since my dad married that psycho bitch. I figured why not?"

"You rebel you," Zee teased.

Neve set the bottle down on the table.

"I've never had wine before," Zee said.

"I had a sip once when I was a kid. My dad let me have a taste," she admitted, smiling at the memory.

"And?"

Neve shrugged. "I didn't hate it."

Zee nodded. She would be willing to give it a try for Neve's sake. She went to the kitchenette and grabbed a couple of glasses. Neve used her knife and popped the bottle open, and then she poured a bit of wine into each glass. Neve took a tiny sip and pulled her face back a little. Zee giggled; she was used to seeing Neve in complete control of her emotions. The Neve in front of her was a little different. Not that it was a bad thing.

"What happened today?" Zee sniffed at her glass.

"What makes you think anything happened today?" Neve met Zee's eyes.

Zee arched an eyebrow and gave Neve a questioning look. "It's two-thirty in the afternoon. I've already had lunch and it's too early for dinner. You're not talking to Bella first, which means you're not ready to have a debate with her right now. Instead, you're here with me with wine. And you said the droids were acting weird. So . . . what happened?"

They sat down and drank the wine while Neve recounted the tale of the morning to Zee.

"Three in one day? All the way out here? That is weird," she said.

"I know, right?"

"What do you think it means?"

"Lila might have something to do with it," Neve replied.

"Your stepmother?"

Neve nodded.

Zee didn't know much about Neve's family history. But she knew enough to know Lila was bad news.

"Not that I'm complaining, but that still doesn't explain why you're here with me," Zee said.

Neve shrugged and looked at the floor. Zee was disarmed by the way Neve was acting. This wasn't her fearless leader; she was more like a woman in love than anything else.

"Today was the first time I was actually worried I wouldn't come back home. I was pretty sure I was screwed. Mostly because I didn't know what would happen next. One zombie? Not a problem. Two? I can handle it. But when the third one showed up and almost bit me, that was when I was genuinely terrified. And you know how some people say your life flashes before your eyes moments before you die?"

Zee nodded. "Yeah."

"All I saw were the faces of the people I loved. People I knew loved me. Like you . . ."

Now that was something Zee hadn't expected to hear. Her heart hammered against her chest so fast it almost hurt. Her stomach was filled with butterflies. Zee removed her glasses and whispered, "What are you saying?"

"I'm saying that life is too short to stand on the sidelines when the right person is standing in front of you."

Before Zee could think of a response, Neve closed the distance between them and kissed her on the lips. Softly at first. Neve then placed her hand on the small of Zee's back and pressed her against her body.

Oh God. I'm dreaming, Zee thought. *I must be dreaming.*

Zee ran her fingers through Neve's short jet-black hair and got lost in the soft, damp locks and deepened their kiss, sending an electric current rushing through her body. As their kiss intensified, Zee quickly came to the happy conclusion that this was very real.

The rest of the afternoon was a blur of hands, sighs, warmth, and skin. In that moment, they were all that existed.

ELEVEN

BELLA OPENED HER EYES. SHE HAD TAKEN A SHORT NAP AND IT HAD done absolutely nothing to make her feel better. She stared at the ceiling while she continued to lie in her bed. She debated whether it was even worth going to the lab. Briar's condition hadn't changed. Her patient was in a stable coma. There was no logical explanation. At least nothing she could recall her mother having taught her. Everything she knew about how to be a doctor and a scientist had been passed on by her mother, Laura. She'd had the opportunity to attend the university and learn and put everything into practice at a hospital before the world was overrun with zombies.

There has to be an explanation, she thought. *Things don't just happen for no good reason.*

Bella sat up and punched the pillow a few times. She hated not having the answer.

"Stupid things I can't solve. I hate it so much," she muttered as she made her bed.

She went to the bathroom, used the toilet, and brushed her teeth. She avoided looking at herself in the mirror. Looking at her reflection was becoming more and more difficult. She wasn't blind. She saw the dark circles under her eyes. How emaciated she was becoming because she often worked straight through her lunch and dinner breaks. She took a deep shaky breath and made a mental checklist of all the things she needed to do that day as she got dressed. She slipped on her dark purple camouflage pants, a long sleeve lavender T-shirt, and a plum-colored vest filled with first aid items like bandages, EpiPens, gauze, and medi-glue.

1. Eat something. Anything.
2. Check in on Briar.
3. Visit Teddy.
4. Try not to cry.
5. Drop off dinner to Jack.
6. Don't fall in love with Jack.

She reminded herself to eat something, so she grabbed a bagel and a cup of coffee from the kitchen and then headed down to the laboratory. Bella went through a series of labyrinthine halls and doors until she finally reached Briar's room. She punched her code into the keypad. The smell of detergent and rubbing alcohol accosted her nostrils. Bella detested that smell, the way it overpowered everything else in the room, to the point that she couldn't even smell her own deodorant. Luckily, she got used to the scent after a few minutes. Good thing she had her coffee with her. Otherwise, she was sure she'd murder someone. Bella set down her mug and bagel on the desk and got to work.

She spent the next few hours checking Briar's pulse, brain waves, blood, skin, and eyes.

Nothing had changed. Not a single thing.

Bella sighed and rested her glasses on top of her head. She massaged her temples and the bridge of her nose. After working nonstop for over a week since Briar had been bitten, she was tired of staring at monitors.

Time to visit Teddy.

Bella went into the room next door and greeted her fiancé in the same cheerful manner she always did. "Hi, Teddy! How are you feeling today?"

The day before she had used a dart gun to inject Teddy with her latest serum. She was hoping to see changes in him since she had injected him with her newest *cure*. She wanted to see how he reacted to it. She turned her camera on and jotted down notes and observations on her chart.

"Unnnghhh," Teddy moaned.

"I know, sweetie. I'm still waiting for the effect of the latest serum to start working on you. Feel anything at the moment?"

"Hungry."

"Ooooh, you're in luck. Neve just got a deer the other day. I'll bring its head down as soon as I can."

Teddy nodded. The chains rattled as he walked toward Bella. That was the only time he moved. The rest of the time he sat in the corner and stared off into space.

As soon as he came to the light, Bella flinched. It was getting harder and harder to see him like this and pretend that it was okay. This was not okay. Nothing about this situation was all right. She wasn't sure how much longer she could do this.

Her messy bun came undone. She needed to redo her hair and readjust the pencils and clips that kept her brown locks in place. Bella pulled the pencils out and undid the messy bun. As she fixed her dark brown hair, she heard the chains move and clink ever so softly. Once everything was in place, she went back to jotting down her observations. Teddy got as close as his bindings would allow and sniffed the air around her. Bella frowned. This was strange.

"You smell . . . different," Teddy muttered.

"Must be some new soap," she lied. She had spent time with Jack since he arrived yesterday. Nothing happened. He had never touched her or vice versa. But Teddy could pick up the subtle change of scent.

Teddy roared and said, "Another man!"

Bella jumped. She pulled the gun out of her holster and aimed it at Teddy's head.

"Who he? Smell . . . on you," he grunted.

Bella had never seen him like this. Jealous. Animated and violent. His red eyes grew darker until they were almost black. His face contorted with rage. He tugged and struggled with his chains as he tried to make his way toward Bella. A layer of his skin peeled back as the chain rubbed against his flesh.

She gasped and pressed herself against the wall behind her. Her hands trembled as she pointed the gun at his head. It was part of her training. Even wearing a blindfold, she could shoot at someone's head if they stood still long enough.

Teddy roared and clawed at the empty space between them. "Teddy, nothing happened." Bella did her best to keep her voice calm. "Not fair!"

"I know, Teddy. I know," she whimpered.

"Can't touch. Can't kiss. Can't love. Can't, can't, can't." He tugged at his chains as he reached out to Bella.

"Teddy, calm down, please. Don't make me hurt you," Bella said.

"Already dead, Bella. Dead." Teddy fell to the floor and folded himself into a fetal position. He placed his hands over his head and whimpered.

A sob escaped her lips. She took a steady breath and focused. Teddy was being crazy, and the last thing she wanted was to get killed because her emotions got in the way.

"Kill me," Teddy said.

He lifted his blood red eyes and locked them with hers. Bella flinched. She couldn't do it. No matter how hard he begged, she could never let him go.

"I can't. You know I can't," she whispered as she lowered the gun.

"Please . . . no more," he begged.

"Dammit, Teddy! I won't do it!" Bella punched her code into the keypad and ran out of the lab. As soon as the door closed behind her, she slid down to the floor and burst into tears.

TWELVE

Sunlight streamed in through the window of Zee's bedroom. A single beam of light landed over Neve's eyes. She let out a happy sigh as she draped her arm over Zee's bare waist. She smiled as she remembered their afternoon of lovemaking. Neve caressed her new lover's hair. Soft. Glinting in the light like a promise.

"Enjoying the view?" Zee whispered.

Neve's cheeks grew warm. "Yeah."

Zee rolled over and propped herself up with her elbow. "Oh my God, you're blushing!" she teased.

Neve covered her face. "Shut up. Don't look at me." She grabbed a pillow and threw it at Zee who caught it and tossed it on the floor.

"It's awesome. I love it."

Neve stuck out her tongue and gave Zee a raspberry.

"Very mature," Zee said.

"All right. Enough happy fun time. I gotta go," Neve said.

"Awww." Zee sat up and pouted.

"Sorry, sweetie. I stayed away way too long. I'll try to come back as soon as possible."

Neve caressed Zee on the cheek and contemplated staying in bed with her. But she had a lot of things to take care of that day. She had to check the compound, talk to Red, check in on Briar's condition, and talk to Jack. Things that couldn't wait a day or two.

"Okay."

Neve leaned over and kissed Zee on the lips.

Neve got dressed and left Zee's apartment. The moment she stepped out of her new sanctuary, she felt the weight of the world back on her shoulders.

She took a deep breath and prepared herself mentally for what was to come.

First on her list was to check in on Jack. He had been in the compound for one day, and he had laid low. She didn't mind. It was one less thing she had to stress about, and she was grateful for it. Her knees buckled as she took the first tentative step away from Zee. But she eventually made her way back to the compound. Back to reality.

Neve knocked on Jack's door and waited.

"Come in," he said. The door opened, and she stepped into his room.

Jack straightened up when he saw Neve. She couldn't explain it. Everyone reacted that way to her. She could already see the positive effect a day of food and rest had on him. He wasn't as pale and emaciated. His eyes were no longer bloodshot, and the dark circles underneath them weren't as pronounced.

"How's everything? Feeling better?"

He nodded. "Much better, thanks."

"I wanted to ask you if you had any skills. Something you're good at."

He quirked his lip. Not quite a smile, not quite a smirk either. "Are you asking me to stay?"

"Maybe."

Jack chuckled. He wiggled his fingers back and forth. "I'm good with my hands. I can fix just about anything."

"How about a garden?" Neve mumbled.

"A garden?" he echoed.

She let out a soft sigh and nodded. "Yeah, ever since Briar's been in a coma," Neve began, "our little nothing of a garden has basically dropped dead on us. No one here but Briar knows a damned thing about plants. We used to have a whole group of people to help. We do the best we can with who we have left here in the compound, but it's not enough."

He rubbed his chin thoughtfully and frowned. "Mind letting me have a look at it?"

"Sure. Follow me."

They made their way to the garden. Before Briar's injury, there had been little pops of green in random places, but in a little over a week, it had turned brown and gray.

"Ooooh, this is bad." Jack let out a low whistle and looked around.

"Yeah . . ." Neve said.

Jack examined the soil and the dried branches that remained. "When I was a kid, I grew a bean in my mom's garden," he said. "It was taller than me. I thought it would reach the sky."

He lifted his gaze to the heavens as though remembering that moment in his life.

"Did it?" Neve shifted her feet.

"Yeah. But I was a kid and pretty short back then, so everything towered over me. We did get a lot of beans from that little plant. I've been gardening ever since. So you could say I have a knack for it."

"Anything you can do to help this garden? Briar and I talked about removing the soil and starting from scratch. But that could take a while."

"Well, I can try to build a small irrigation system. I'll just need a few things. We'll also have to change the fertilizer. Whatever your friend was using wasn't working anymore." He picked up a handful of soil and rubbed it between his fingers until it fell back on the ground. "It'll take a bit of work. I can't make any promises, but I'll try."

"Thank you. You are welcome to stay so long as you work and do your part. Nothing is handed out to anyone here."

His blue eyes had a glint of hope and he gave her a genuine smile. "Really?"

"Yeah. Just don't do anything to piss me off. I'd hate to chop off something you'll miss," Neve said.

Jack let out a nervous chuckle. "Gotcha."

Neve tossed him a pair of gloves; he caught them with his left hand with ease.

"Do I really have to wear these?"

"I don't know. Ask Briar. She wasn't wearing them when the snake infected with the virus almost ripped her fingers off."

"Gloves on at all times. Got it," Jack replied as he slipped them on.

"So? Is there any hope?"

He scratched the back of his neck and looked around. "At least you've been watering it. So that's a good thing. But I'll figure it out. Anyway . . . who's this Briar I've been hearing about?"

"She's a good friend of mine. Mouth like a seasoned truck driver but kind. Tougher than she looks. People have made the mistake of underestimating her and lived to regret it. So when she wakes up from her coma, watch your step."

"She didn't turn?" He had an awestruck look on his face.

Neve didn't blame him. Anyone bitten by a zombie turned almost immediately. That Briar had gone a little over a week without changing into a monster spoke volumes of her resilience and strength.

"Nope."

"So . . . she's been basically . . . sleeping this whole time?"

"Yep."

"Weird," Jack whispered.

"Yep."

"What happened with the snake?" he asked.

"Red and Gus burned the head and body. It's been taken care of. But keep your gloves on and have a knife on you at all times. I'm not kidding. It could literally be the difference between life and death."

Jack nodded. "Anything else I ought to know?"

"You'll learn the rules as you go along. If you have any questions, feel free to ask me or anyone else in the compound."

"All right."

Neve wasn't sure she was doing the right thing having him here, but she wanted to give him a chance. She just hoped it wouldn't be a decision she would regret.

Neve went to the gun range and found Red. Charles had it built to practice and stay up to par with all of the weapons in the compound. Naturally, Red was the one who used this room the most.

She currently used a .270 Winchester rifle to fire at the blank-faced target in the distance as though it had murdered her entire family. For all Neve knew, her friend was probably imagining it had.

Her bright red short hair could be seen from a mile away. The room boomed with every shot she fired from her gun.

"Hey Red!" Neve cried. She wanted to make sure that Red knew she was in the room. The last thing she wanted was to startle Red and get shot.

"What do you want?"

"Don't forget I need you and Gus to come with me tomorrow morning."

Red turned around. There was a glint in her blue eye. She had a wicked grin on her lips. "How could I? You fucked up."

"Yeah."

"Am I allowed to bring Ajax?"

Neve looked down at Red's half-wolf, half-Siberian husky. The thing was half as tall as she was. "Of course, Ajax can come."

"He'll behave, don't worry. At least until a zombie shows up. He'll have fun ripping its head off."

Neve chuckled.

"Can I bring Velma, too?"

"You probably won't need her," Neve said.

Red feigned a gasp and placed a hand over her chest. "I'm gonna tell her you said that."

"Keep it light, Red. We're not planning an invasion or anything like that. We're just going to check things out and burn the bodies I left behind. That's all."

Red pursed her lips and shook her head. "You're a spoil sport. You never let me have any fun."

"You're not bringing a rocket launcher with us," Neve argued.

Red narrowed her eye and arched an eyebrow. "Velma is a not a rocket launcher. She's an M203 grenade launcher. You'd know if I had a rocket launcher. I probably would've blown up half the place by now."

"Yeah . . . still not bringing her."

"Fine," Red spat.

"You'll thank me later."

"And you'll be sorry," Red said in a singsong tone.

"I doubt it," Neve said.

"Bright and early tomorrow then?"

"Yep."

"Why don't we go now?" Red asked.

"Because it's a long ways away and I'm exhausted. I think it'll be all right for it to wait one day," Neve said.

"Okay." Red turned around and went back to her target practice. Not like she needed it. She could hit every target blindfolded. All of the heads on the blank targets were blown off by the time Neve made it to the door.

If it was something Red excelled at, it was killing zombies. It was how she had survived the first time they had attacked her town. She was never the same after she lost her grandmother and her eye that day. Red had become obsessed with guns and making sure she knew how each one worked. And how to keep them clean. They all had names, but her favorite was Velma.

Neve was glad Red was on their side and living in the compound. If they ever went to war, Neve wanted Red on her side.

Red watched Neve walk away. She frowned for a moment. There was something different about Neve lately. She seemed . . . softer. Not so rough around the edges and ready to snap like normal. Red didn't know what to make of it. She should shrug it off and leave Neve alone. Whatever it was, she was sure Neve had a good handle on it. In the five years she had been living in The Orchard, Neve had never let her down.

She leaned down and gave Ajax a soft scratch under his chin. Her dog was already used to Red's rifles and guns, so he wasn't bothered by the sound of gunfire. She checked her targets and was pleased to see she had hit the bullseye every single time. She knew there was no real need for her to practice so much. Even with one eye, she was a better marksman than everyone in the compound.

Red left the gun range and spotted Neve in the storage room.

She pressed her back against the wall and snuck a peek.

Neve reached for a DVD and popcorn.

A movie? She couldn't remember the last time she had seen Neve relax with a movie, let alone popcorn. Neve was as straitlaced as they came. She was always staying up late reading or patrolling. The only thing Neve did was work.

Unless . . .

Red smiled and walked away as quietly as possible. "Ajax, this is unprecedented," she whispered.

Her pet gave her a blank stare.

"I know. I'm wondering the same thing," Red said.

Ajax gave her a doggy grin and let his tongue hang out.

"No way it's Gus. Because he's with me, and he knows I'd chop his dick off if I ever caught him cheating. Not Jack. He's new here. It takes years for Neve to trust anyone."

Ajax let out a soft whimper.

"Nah. Not Sam. He's not her type. Or Will . . . even though he'd eat a fried boot for her."

Red and Ajax made it to her room, and she flopped onto her bed. She continued to run through the list of potential lovers for Neve. None of them seemed like the right one.

"I dunno Ajax. Maybe I'm wrong. Maybe Neve just needed popcorn and a movie," she said as she ran her fingers over Ajax's soft fur.

"Do you think we should follow her?"

Ajax lay down and covered his eyes with his paws.

"Awww. Come on. It'll be fun," Red said.

Ajax whimpered.

"Ugh. Fine. I'll go by myself."

Her dog barked in protest and jumped up.

"That a boy! Let's go." Red ran out the door with Ajax following closely beside her.

Red hid behind a bush and searched for Neve, but her fearless leader had vanished. Red frowned and scratched the top of her head.

"Where is she?" she whispered.

Her dog sniffed the air and ran out of her hiding place.

That can't be right. Her room is on the other side of the compound near the front gate. She followed Ajax until they were in front of Zee's tower.

"Are you sure?" she whispered.

Ajax barked and spun around a few times.

"She's probably bringing something to her then. My mistake, I think."

Red walked away none the wiser.

On her way back to her room, she saw Jack walk into the kitchen out of the corner of her good eye.

"Howdy stranger," Red said as she followed him. He gasped in surprise and turned to face her.

"Hi. Umm . . . I'm sorry. I was hungry. And Bella hasn't come by to bring me anything to eat," he explained.

"It's all right. Kitchen is a free for all. We all take turns cleaning and stocking the cabinets to make sure there's always something in here for everyone.

We usually stay out of each other's rooms and respect each other's privacy as long as it doesn't harm anyone else in the compound."

"But Neve is still pretty strict."

Red rested her back against the wall and crossed her arms over her chest. "Can't say I blame her. She's been in charge of this place since she was a teenager. Anything bad that happens here is her fault. Even if it isn't, she takes full responsibility. So that's why she comes across like such a ball buster. And we're here to enforce her rules."

Jack nodded.

"Lucky for you, I'm on break," Red lied. She was always ready for action. But she wanted to know more about Jack and why he was here. She would be his friend . . . for now.

"I'm gonna grab a snack for later. Did you need help finding anything?"

"Maybe some soup?" he replied. "Or anything really. I'm hungry—basically making up for weeks with little food and water."

"I hear ya. The canned goods are in the pantry. That big door next to the fridge. We also have crackers in the cabinet over there," she said and pointed to that general area.

"Perfect. Thank you so much," he said.

Red helped him find his way around the kitchen. She found a bowl and pointed out a few other things in the kitchen. "The utensils are in this drawer by the toaster. And the big button in the microwave gets stuck sometimes." She pressed the yellowed button that opened the microwave door. And just as she said, it got stuck. "It's old, and beggars can't be choosers. So you have to press it on the corners, not the middle otherwise it won't work," Red explained.

"Big button on the corners. Gotcha," he whispered. Jack looked around the kitchen and muttered everything Red said to himself as though memorizing every single thing she said for future reference.

"Anything else?" she asked.

He shook his head. "No. I think I'm good."

"Okay. I'll leave you to it," she said.

"Thanks again," Jack said.

Red nodded and then walked out of the kitchen with Ajax by her side. She was surprised that he hadn't barked or growled at him. Ajax was still vigilant but relatively relaxed around Jack.

Interesting . . . very interesting . . .

Dogs tended to know firsthand if someone was trustworthy or not. Even though Red was still on the fence about Jack, she trusted Ajax's initial instinct.

THIRTEEN

NEVER HAD FUN WITH ZEE THAT EVENING. THEY STAYED UP LATE watching a movie about toys that came to life and tried to find their way back home. It was sweet and funny. She couldn't remember the last time she'd had such a good time. But she didn't spend the night in Zee's tower. She needed to go back to her cold and lonely room to prepare herself mentally for the next day. It was time to go back to reality and make up for the mistake in the forest.

She woke up early, got her things packed and was ready to get started. Neve chastised herself for her mistake of leaving the zombie bodies. She should've taken one of their trucks after she'd returned with the deer and driven up to the woods to burn them.

She stood by the front gate waiting for Red and Gus to show up. She thought about Zee as she lovingly gazed up at her tower. She was a delightful distraction; falling in love was the strangest thing that had ever happened to Neve. She wasn't sure if there was a right or wrong way to do it. But today she needed to get her head out of the clouds and back into taking care of her friends.

She was about to call Red and Gus on the communicator when she saw Red walking toward her.

Neve frowned. Something looked a little . . . off. Literally.

"Oh geez. What. The. Fuck?" Neve hissed. She came to the shocking realization that Red was topless. "Seriously?"

"What?" Red asked, feigning innocence. Ajax whimpered and covered his face with his paws.

"Put a shirt on, please," Neve ordered.

"I didn't bring one. It took up too much room in my bag, and you said travel light," Red replied. She pushed her chest outward as she yawned. Her dark pink nipples perked up as a breeze caressed her bare skin.

"Not that light," Neve cried.

Red gave her an impish smirk and shrugged playfully.

Neve groaned loudly and shook her head. "I have an extra shirt, hang on."

Neve forced herself to look away. She hoped Zee wasn't paying too much attention to what was happening right now. The last thing she wanted to do was make Zee jealous.

Gus walked up and chuckled when he saw Red. "I had a feeling that today was gonna be a good day," he said.

"Oh, shut up," Neve said as she rummaged through her backpack.

Red motioned at her exposed breasts with her hands. "You say that as if I had ugly boobs or something. Like I should have a reason to cover them up. Lucky for you, I have bodacious tatas, and Gus isn't complaining."

"It's insanely distracting. And Gus is a guy, his opinion on this doesn't count. Exhibit A." Neve pointed to Gus's crotch. The man was sporting an impressive erection.

"It's not distracting," Red argued.

"This was a bad idea. You're staying here."

Gus cleared his throat. "Umm . . . I don't mind if she comes."

"You'll cum in your pants while a zombie gnaws on your brains." Neve pulled out an olive-green T-shirt and handed it to Red. "Here, put this on. We don't have time for this shit."

"Spoil sport," Red muttered. She put the T-shirt on without another word. It hung a little loose on Red, but at least she was covered.

"I second that," Gus said.

"Yeah, yeah. Piss all over me if you want. I'm the only one keeping all you sons of bitches alive. You can thank me later," Neve said.

Red giggled.

Neve knew Red loved pushing her buttons and getting under her skin just for fun.

"All right, you weirdoes, let's go," Neve said.

Together, they left the compound. She sent her droids ahead to scout the area as always.

"We should've taken the truck," Gus said as they walked over the bridge.

"We're saving it for an emergency," Neve said.

"This doesn't count?" Gus asked.

"Nope. This is recon. An emergency would be if there were hundreds of zombies surrounding the compound, and we need to get the fuck out of here in one piece."

Gus sighed, which let Neve know she had won that argument. If she had limitless amounts of gasoline and fuel, she would use the truck for everything. She would use it to drive to the kitchen, to the bathroom, everywhere. She would basically refuse to walk unless absolutely necessary.

They walked and chatted amicably as they made their way back into the woods. Neve shook her head whenever Red and Gus flirted playfully with each other. They were in their own little world.

"Wow. Look at all this greenery." Red's voice rose in awe as she looked around.

"Yeah. It caught me by surprise, too," Neve said.

"This is where you caught that deer?" Gus gazed at the lushness.

Neve nodded. She was on high alert now that they were closer to where she had been attacked. She readied her weapons, and Red and Gus followed her lead. Ajax sniffed the soil as they continued to explore the forest. Neve had her droids scouting the area as well. Ha-P zipped past them, singing his cheerful tune as always.

So far . . . nothing.

Neve did her best to remember the path she had taken the day before. After a few minutes of searching, they found the exact spot where she had been attacked. Two of the three dead zombies had flies swirling around their carcasses.

Gus narrowed his eyes and shot Neve a look. She knew what he would say before he even opened his mouth.

"You didn't burn them? You know that's just going to attract more of them here," Gus said.

She had *forgotten* to tell Gus the mistake she'd made for this exact reason. She'd dreaded the look of disappointment on his face.

"I'm sorry," she said. "I had a dead deer I needed to bring home, and to be completely honest . . . I was alone and scared. Is that what you wanna hear?"

Gus took a deep breath. He knew it cost Neve a lot to admit that to them out loud.

"That's why we're here," Neve said.

She felt her chest burn with shame. She should've known better; she was getting sloppy. Mistakes were what got people killed. Neve shook those thoughts out of her head.

"It's only been a little over a day. Hopefully, it's nothing and didn't draw attention," she said.

Gus grunted in response. Red put her bags down and looked around the area with Ajax. She was often lost in her own world, so Neve let her wander off. Ajax was good at keeping her in check if she went a little too crazy.

Neve walked up to Gus and took a deep breath. "I'm sorry," she whispered.

"It's all right. We're here now," he replied.

"It's not all right. I should've fucking known better," Neve said.

"You're distracted," Gus said. He pulled a bottle of lighter fluid from his pocket and poured it over the two dead bodies.

"That obvious, huh?"

"Yeah. You don't scowl as much," he said.

Neve smirked and shook her head. Gus chuckled and pulled out a box of matches. "So . . ."

"So what?" Neve wiped the smile from her face.

"Who is he?"

"He?" Neve arched an eyebrow.

Gus struck the match and took a step backwards as he dropped it onto the pile of zombies.

"Yeah. Your fella," he said.

"Not a *he*," she said unable to suppress her grin.

"Ooooh . . . you found yourself a girl," Gus said.

"Yeah."

"Should I guess or are you gonna tell me?"

The wind blew the flames away. Gus struck another match and dropped it again. This time it caught fire. Neve gagged as the smell of rotten sulfur reached her nostrils. She pulled her shirt over her nose to try to mask the scent. It didn't help in the slightest, but it gave her a moment to stall. The odor eventually died down a few moments later, and she could breathe normally again.

"Zee," Neve said.

"Zee?" he echoed.

"Yeah. She's my lady love."

Gus' eyebrows shot up in surprise. "Wow. Excellent choice by the way. The American dream, huh? Find a nice girl, settle down, get a house with a white picket fence. Have two point five children?"

"Thanks. Definitely found a nice girl. Don't know about the picket fence thing. Maybe a nine foot gate to keep zombies out of our house. Kids? Not so sure about that," she said.

"I just hope we don't die because you're distracted by pussy," he said with a chuckle as the flames engulfed the two zombies.

She gave him a playful shove. "Fuck you, man. You're one to talk. You've been fucking every girl at The Orchard since you got your first chest hair."

"Yeah. But I'm not the one in charge of everyone," he teased.

"Anything else you wanna say, smart-ass?"

"Nah. Just messin' with you. I'm happy for you. Zee's cool."

"Thanks. I think so, too," she said.

He took a deep breath and looked around. "Anyway, back to business. Any other zombies out here you forgot to incinerate?"

"There should be one more not far from here," she said. "Let's go burn it up then."

Gus and Neve headed deeper into the woods in search of the other zombie when she heard Ajax bark. The dog then growled loudly enough to make the hairs on the back of her neck stand on end.

"That can't be good," Neve muttered as she raced toward the sound.

Gus followed closely behind her.

"Whoa!" Neve shouted as she skidded to a halt. Gus ran into her and almost knocked her over.

Red had killed a female zombie and was currently lost in her own world as she bludgeoned its head to a pulp with the hilt of her shotgun.

"Red! Red, snap out of it," Neve said.

She took a step toward her, but Gus grabbed her arm and pulled her back.

"You don't wanna do that," he said. "We wait for her to relax enough for someone to gently bring her back to the present. Usually Ajax is the best one to help her snap out of it. But from the looks of it, she might be too far gone."

"Okay," Neve said.

It was obvious that Gus would have to take the lead with this. He and Red were romantically involved, and they were always together. He knew how to bring Red back from the labyrinthine depths of her mind.

"Stupid motherfuckers! Why won't you die?" Red shouted as she beat the zombie some more. Ajax snapped its jaws at the zombie and snarled.

Red kicked and stomped on the female zombie's head a few more times. Her boots and legs were covered with the zombie's blue-black blood. Neve flinched when she heard the deafening crunch of the zombie's skull cracking.

After what felt like an eternity, Red's shoulders relaxed. She took a deep, shaky breath and dropped her shotgun. She had a thin layer of sweat all over her skin and gasped for air a few times. She looked as though she had just finished running a marathon.

Gus carefully approached her, making sure his hands were visible.

"Red?" he whispered.

She shouted in surprise when she saw him. Red narrowed her eye for a second, as if trying to decipher who he was.

"It's me . . . Gus," he said in a gentle voice. He held his hand out to Ajax, who licked it a few times. "See? Ajax knows me. We're friends."

Red frowned. "We are?"

Gus nodded.

"I have to find Granny. She's all alone and needs me," she said in a soft, almost child-like voice.

"Okay. We'll go together," he said.

Red gingerly touched her eyepatch, and then she screamed in horror, shaking her head as though trying to put everything back into place inside her mind. "Gus?" she whispered.

"Yeah. It's me. I'm here."

Red looked around. Her fingers softly touched her lips. "I didn't hurt anyone . . . did I?"

"Don't worry. I'm sure that zombie you beat to a pulp had it comin'," he said.

"Are you all right?" Neve stepped forward.

Red gave her a shaky nod. "I just need a minute."

Gus quickly pulled out a wipe and cleaned Red's face as best as he could. Red tilted her head up and let him fuss over her. He used a lighter and burned the wipe. It vanished in a puff of smoke before it reached the ground.

"Okay. I'll be with the other dead zombie. We should add that one to the list," Neve walked away and gave them a moment of privacy. She would talk to Bella to see if there was a way to recreate Red's medication. She needed her friend to be okay.

Neve eventually found the zombie she'd left behind in the woods and doused it with lighter fluid. She struck a match and took a step back as she dropped it on top of the carcass. As she watched the flames engulf its body, she wondered who he used to be before he became infected with the Aetervia virus. Was he someone's husband? Doctor? Teacher? Mechanic?

She wondered if he had been all alone in the world with no one to mourn his loss. All so he could die twice in the middle of the woods. Maybe he had attacked Neve because he knew that was the only way he would finally be at peace.

She sat there and watched him burn.

Neve pressed the blue button on her shoulder and called her droids to return. She waited a few moments and as usual, D.O.C. was the first one to come back. She picked it up and looked at the pictures. Her eyes widened in shock and she almost dropped her precious droid.

"Holy fucking shit," Neve whispered.

"What?" Gus made his way into the clearing. Neve covered her mouth and shook her head.

Gus took D.O.C. and looked at the images. "Fuck," he hissed.

"Let me guess . . . zombies. Lots of them?" Red joined them.

"Yeah," Neve replied.

"Well . . . what the fuck are we waiting for? Let's go. That's why we're here ladies." Red dug around her duffel bag and pulled out her grenade launcher.

"You brought Velma?" Neve asked.

Red laughed and caressed her weapon as she would a lover. She licked her lips seductively and placed a tender kiss on Velma. "I sure did."

"Is it weird that I'm turned on by this?" Gus whispered.

"No," Neve replied.

Gus gave her a wide grin. "All right. Let's do this."

"D.O.C., show us where they are," Neve said.

D.O.C. chirped and flew toward the zombies he had photographed. Together they followed the droid.

"Holy. Fucking. Shit," Neve said when they reached the bright green field. There were at least two dozen zombies ambling toward them. Their rotten flesh dangling off their bones as they gnashed their teeth.

Red knelt and readied Velma. While Red assembled her grenade launcher with expert precision, Neve and Gus aimed their weapons and fired at every zombie on sight.

"Are you done?" Neve snapped.

"Yep! Move!" Red roared. "Eat my shit, you fuckers!" She pulled the trigger on Velma. With that shot alone, Red decimated five zombies.

While Red reloaded her weapon, Neve and Gus got to work with the other zombies that had come close enough. Neve alternated between using her shotgun and hacking away at the zombies with her trusty machete. Gus used his rifle. Together, they took down seven zombies. Her arms ached halfway through the battle, but there was no way in hell she would slow down. It gave Red time to run back and reload from a safe distance.

Only twelve to go, she thought as she pulled the trigger and watched as the round blew off the right side of a male zombie's face. It fell on the ground with a loud thud.

"Ready!" Red shouted.

Neve and Gus ran behind her and covered their heads. Red cackled with delight as she fired another grenade at the hoard of zombies. That shot took down another group of five. Neve and Gus ran up and killed the remaining seven. Her machete was drenched with their blue-black blood. She watched as a few drops fell to the ground with a soft splat staining the green grass beneath her feet. Death and decay seemed to follow her wherever she went.

When the last zombie fell to the ground Neve let out a sigh of relief. This was unprecedented. Even the scent of three dead zombies shouldn't have been enough to attract twenty-four zombies. Two maybe. Especially with how remote they were.

"What. The. Actual. Fuck." Neve said.

"Ditto," Red said.

Gus wiped the sweat that trickled down his forehead with the back of his hand and nodded in agreement.

"I hope we have enough lighter fluid to burn these fuckers," Red said.

"We'll make it work," Neve said. "We'll just douse the ones in the perimeter and hope it catches. If not, we'll gather wood and do what we can. But we're not leaving until they're all burned into a pile of ashes."

"Agreed," Gus said.

Neve and Gus poured lighter fluid over the zombies, and she came to a complete stop when she saw a familiar face. It was the nose that she recognized right away. Long and round, almost like someone had glued a small eggplant in the middle of his face. She stared at him until she remembered that his name was Michael Gildred. Before she could stop herself, she knelt down and rummaged through his clothes. She gagged at the smell of rot and decay that overpowered her senses, but she continued rummaging through his things. She was surprised to find that he still had his wallet on him. Usually, those were the first things to fall out of men's pockets when they turned.

She stepped away from the pile of dead bodies and checked his wallet. She found his ID card. The one issued to him by her father fifteen years ago, around the time the building of The Orchard was complete. She couldn't believe he still had it after all this time.

"Son of a bitch," she hissed.

"What? What's wrong?" Red asked.

"Nothing. Just . . . someone I knew once upon a time," Neve said.

"Doesn't sound like you liked him all that much," Red muttered.

Neve ignored Red and kept looking through his wallet. She found a white card (or at least it had been white a long time ago) and in big black letters it said Beauchamp Laboratories. There was a square chip, much more sophisticated than what her father had in his card so many years ago.

"You motherfucker," she whispered. Neve kicked Michael's head and didn't stop until his skull caved in. She yanked her bloodied boot out of his skull and yelled in frustration.

The ID was issued last year. That meant that the fucking bitch was still out there somewhere. She read the card over and over again until she memorized the address on the back of the card.

"Who is he?" Red asked.

"An old friend of my father's," Neve said.

"Whoa. Must not have been that good a friend," Red said.

"Yeah."

"Poor guy. I wonder how he ended up this way."

"Chasing after Lila. He was in love with her. Stupid dick," Neve said.

"I'm sorry," Red said.

"He should've stayed here with us."

"Do you want me to burn him with the rest?"

"Yeah," Neve said in a cold, detached voice. She hated the way she sounded, but this wasn't her father's friend anymore. It was a monster that had gnashed its teeth at her, searching for something warm to feast upon.

"Cool," Red said.

This was Red's favorite part, setting them on fire. "I call dibs on any jewelry."

"You can do whatever the fuck you want. I ain't wearing no dead person's stuff," Gus said as he walked over to Neve.

"Gus, take a look at this," Neve said as she showed him Michael's ID.

"What the fuck?"

"Yeah. I thought the same exact thing," she said.

Gus was one of the few people who had been at the compound since day one. He knew exactly who Michael was and what he had done. Gus gave Michael's corpse a dirty look and kicked the dead body in the crotch.

"Stupid fucker. This is all his fault," Gus growled as he kept kicking.

"Feeling better?" Neve raised a brow.

"No," he replied and then gave him one final, hard kick.

"Now?"

"Still no, but I'll stop," he said.

It took them several hours to gather and burn all of the zombies including Michael. They wanted to avoid another mistake like the one Neve had made. Sweat trickled down her temples as she took a deep breath and lifted her gaze up to the sky. It had turned into a series of colors: pink, lavender, and indigo blue. All of it a beautiful ombre that made it difficult for Neve to look away. It was amazing that there could still be something pretty to look at even among all of the chaos and death that surrounded them every single day. Strangely, it made her feel hopeful for the future.

Eventually, she forced herself to look away. They needed to be back at the compound before dark. There was no way of knowing what they would encounter on their way home.

"All right, let's go," Neve said.

Gus and Red both nodded and followed her lead. Neve programmed D.O.C. to go ahead and scout the area. The other droids lighted the way like little miners with their lanterns softly swinging from side to side. Together, they started the long trek home. All the while Neve wondered about Michael and the path he had chosen. Out of all the people to trust, he had put his faith in Lila. Another fool blinded by love.

Was the same thing happening to her? Would she be so enamored with Zee that she wouldn't be able to see the truth? She shook her head. Knowing Zee, she would knock sense into her the moment she saw anything out of the ordinary. Zee was her True North.

Zee is my happy ever after.

With that thought in her mind, she smiled as they got closer to the compound. Zee's tower was already within her line of sight.

Those words rang truer with every step she took.

THE FOLLOWING MORNING, NEVE WAS IN THE KITCHEN MAKING HERself a cup of ginger tea and some toast with butter. Yesterday's events were still weighing on her mind. She had cleaned all of Michael's IDs, and they were currently burning a hole in her pocket. She had to force herself to keep them there. Otherwise, she would stare at them all day long.

Red walked into the kitchen with Bella trailing behind her. Bella looked exhausted, as though she hadn't had a good night's sleep in weeks. Her eyes were bloodshot.

"Morning," Red said.

"Morning," Neve echoed.

Bella walked right past her in a bit of a daze. Red sat down next to Neve and watched the interaction between the two best friends.

"Bella? Are you okay?" Neve ventured.

Bella flinched and pressed her back against the wall. Her hand went to her chest, as though trying to keep her heart from bursting out of her ribcage.

"Whoa. It's just me. Calm down," Neve said.

Bella closed her eyes and tucked a loose strand of her brown hair behind her ear. When she opened them, they still looked bloodshot. "I'm sorry. I didn't see you there."

"Are you okay? What's going on with you?"

"I'm fine. Just working too hard."

"Bella . . ." Neve warned.

"I've been staying up late because I think I'm close to a breakthrough," Bella said, desperation in her voice. "But I don't wanna say too much in case I'm wrong. I don't want to jinx this."

"Okay. But promise me you'll get some sleep tonight. And yes, I will go to your room to check," Neve said.

"You know she's not going to do that," Red whispered.

"Yeah. I promise," Bella replied.

Red leaned forward and in a mock whisper said, "She's not going to sleep. She's going to stay up all night working."

"I will lock her in her room if I have to," Neve said.

"Stop talking about me as if I'm not in the room," Bella said. She made herself a quick bowl of oatmeal and walked out of the kitchen.

"She's going to work herself to death," Red said

"I hope not. I wish she would just kill Teddy and be done with that nonsense."

"You know as well as I do that she's not going to rest until she finds a cure. She loves Teddy too much to let him go."

Neve sighed and took a bite of her toast. She knew better than to argue with Red. She always had something to counter with, and today, she wasn't in the mood.

"Do you think there are more zombies out there?" Red took a bite of her food.

"I don't know," Neve whispered, pulling out Michael's ID card.

"Maybe we should ask Jack," Red suggested.

"Jack?"

"Yeah. Maybe he'll recognize Michael's picture. Maybe he ran away from their lab," Red said.

"That's a good idea. I'll do just that."

Neve got up and made her way out the door.

"Wait. Right now?" Red scrambled to her feet and followed Neve.

"No time like the present." Neve turned on her communicator. "Zee?"

"Morning, Sweetie. What do you need?" Zee crooned.

"You know what I need," Neve said.

"Oooh. I'm always here for you when you're ready for more," Zee purred.

Neve blushed and tried to hide her smile from Red. And failed.

"But unfortunately for us . . . you're looking for Jack. He's in the garden," Zee said.

Red grabbed Neve by the arm and held her back. "Think this through."

"What? This was your idea." Neve pulled her arm out of Red's grip.

"I know, but don't be so fucking impulsive . . . for once. We might get him to trust us and just see if he'll talk if we don't go barrels blazin'."

Neve sighed.

"She has a point," Zee chimed in.

"Okay. Fine. I'll talk to him . . . nicely."

"You should try saying that without rolling your eyes so much. I dunno. Maybe you should let Bella talk to him. Nice comes naturally to her," Red said as she scratched her freckled nose.

"Bella is distracted and exhausted right now. Besides, I can be nice if I want," Neve argued.

"Sure." Red teased.

"You're nice to me," Zee said.

Neve groaned. "All right. We're done here." Neve turned off the communicator and narrowed her eyes at Red.

"Are you going to ask Bella to talk to him?"

"No. I'm going to prove to you I can be nice," Neve said.

Red threw her head back and cackled. Ajax barked playfully and spun around a few times, as though enjoying that Red was happy. She wiped a tear from her eye and gasped for air. "Oh man. I needed that."

"Fuck you."

"Nice. That was really, really nice. I wonder what else you'll do today."

"Ugh. Go away." Neve walked to the garden.

"Hell no! I'm following you. I've always wanted to see a train wreck in person. I want to look away . . . but I can't do it. No matter how hard I try."

Neve went to the garden and found Jack hard at work. Tilling the soil, adding fertilizer and doing his best to bring the plot of dirt back to life. He was keeping his promise to her. He took a momentary break to stretch and wipe the sweat off his forehead and the bridge of his nose.

"Oh! Hey, I didn't see you there," Jack said, giving them a warm smile.

"Sorry. Didn't mean to startle you. Everything okay?" Neve smiled.

Red crossed her arms over her chest and rested her back against the wall. She was there for voyeuristic purposes alone.

"Yeah. Just working on the garden like you asked me to. Is something wrong?"

He looked at her with those haunting blue eyes. Where did she know him from? She stared at him for a moment longer than she had intended and quickly forced herself to look away. Even though she wanted to trust him, there was just something slightly off about him.

Neve took a deep breath. She would keep her thinly veiled rage in check for once . . . if only to prove a point. "I was hoping that you could help me figure something out," Neve said.

Jack nodded.

Be nice, Neve repeated like a mantra. She pulled the ID card out of her pocket and handed it to Jack. "Do you recognize this man?"

He held the card and stared at it for a long time. His hands trembled as he handed the card back to her.

"Ummm . . . h–how did you get this?" he whispered.

"We were attacked by a hoard of zombies while we were out in the woods cleaning up my mess," Neve explained.

Jack looked several shades paler, like he would throw up right there in the garden. Neve took a step back just in case. The last thing she wanted was to get vomit all over her clothes. He took a deep breath and ran his hand over his face. "I do know him. Or at least I knew him while he was alive. We lived at the same compound for a while before I left."

Neve could tell he wasn't giving her the complete truth. What was he hiding? "What is your real name?"

"I told you it's Jack . . ."

"No, it's not. What is it really?" she pressed.

"Jonathan . . . Jonathan Beauchamp," he said, finally relenting.

Neve clenched her jaw so hard that she thought she would break her teeth. Same last name as Lila. Was he her nephew? Her brother?

"I told you Jack was a fucking nickname," she said to Red. "How were you able to erase your information from the computer? Everyone is in the system." Zee still hadn't been able to find anything on him with the blood sample she had.

"You're not the only one with a hacker," Jack said.

"Where exactly was your compound?" she asked.

"Northern Texas."

"You walked from Texas all the way here?"

"I told you. There were zombies attacking us almost every day. What I told Bella about my pregnant girlfriend was true."

"Why are you here?" Neve demanded. Jack remained silent.

Neve looked back at Red and arched an eyebrow. Her red-headed friend gave her a single nod, as though giving her permission to drop the act.

Neve punched him in the jaw and grabbed a fistful of Jack's hair. She pulled him close to her and shouted in his ear, "Why are you here?"

Jack coughed for a moment and spat a bit of blood on the ground. He let out a painful groan and shook his head. "I heard about this place. I wanted to see if it was real. I wanted to see if I could find it," he said.

"From who? Why?"

"I lied to you," Jack whispered.

"About more than your name? What else did you lie about?" Neve released the vice-like grip she had on him.

He fell to the ground and rubbed his jaw. He coughed a few more times and brought himself to a seated position on the ground. "About why I left my old compound."

"You said it was because of your pregnant girlfriend and the zombie attacks."

Jack coughed and wiped blood that trickled from the corner of his lip. "Yes, but that wasn't the only reason I came looking for you and this place."

He pulled out a picture from his back pocket and handed it to Neve. She took it from his hand and unfolded it. Her heart dropped to her stomach when she saw the image. A much younger Lila held a two-year-old Jack in her arms. They had the same big blue eyes and high cheek bones. Lila's lips were small, but had a perfect cupid's bow shape. Her brown hair had a bronze-like sheen and it reached the small of her back. She couldn't have been more than eighteen years old when the photograph was taken. Young Jack had short blonde hair and chubby cheeks. He wore a green T-shirt with blue overalls and white tennis shoes. But the smile on his face was reserved for his mother.

Lila was looking at Jack as if he had placed the sun in the sky. Neve had never seen her look at anyone like that . . . ever. Not even her father.

This version of her stepmother wasn't the one Neve had met when she was thirteen years old. The woman in this picture was smiling, joyful . . . happy. Where had that woman gone? How had Lila become the obsessive, mad scientist who had invaded her home so many years ago? The one who was hell bent on getting her beauty back at all costs?

"She's your mother?" Neve felt the acidic taste of bile tickle the back of her throat.

Jack nodded.

"Is that why you're here? To spy on us? To gather information and give it to your evil bitch of a mother?" Neve took a step forward, ready to deck him again.

Jack shook his head. "No. I swear I was just trying to get away from her. I figured this was the last place on Earth she would think to look. You don't know what it's like to live with her."

"Yes . . . I do."

Darkness filled Jack's blue eyes as he glanced up at Neve. "Whatever you think you know about my mother, trust me, it's just the tip of the iceberg. You don't know a thing about that monster."

A sudden chill came over Neve. Without realizing she had done so, she rubbed her arms to warm herself up.

"So what now?" Neve crossed her arms.

"I don't know. I can't . . . I don't want to go," he whispered.

"This makes you being here much more complicated. I don't want anyone to get hurt because you're hiding from your mother."

"I'm not gonna beg. But I will do anything . . . anything if you let me stay here."

Neve looked away. She couldn't stand to look into his eyes. Now that she knew who he was, she realized that they were the same shade of blue as his mother's. How had she not realized it sooner? She turned her gaze back at him. He rubbed his jaw and wiped the excess blood off his skin.

Would she really punish someone who was innocent?

Someone trying to escape his own house of horrors? She wondered . . . what would her father have done?

"I'll think about it," she whispered.

Neve walked past Red and out of the garden.

Red chased after Neve. "Wait. That's it? That's all you're going to do?"

"That was me being nice. What more do you want?" Neve said.

"He's the son of the woman you hate more than anything in the world. You're just going to let him stay? He lied! He lied about who he was. You're just going to believe him now?"

Neve took a shaky breath and tried to rub the sting of tears out of her eyes. Her hand still throbbed from punching him.

"I kick him out and then what? What does that prove? What good is it going to do anyone?" Neve whispered.

"Love is making you soft, my friend," Red replied.

"And if it is? Is that such a bad thing? When did having a soft heart become such a bad thing? I'm tired, Red. I'm so tired of being strong all the time. Maybe . . . just maybe Jack will be the one who helps us put everything to an end."

"What do you mean everything?" Red asked.

"The virus. Humanity. Life. All of it. Who knows?"

Red shook her head. "I don't know," she whispered.

"Neither do I."

FOURTEEN

Jack woke up early the next day. He groaned as he sat up on his bed. His jaw was still sore from the wallop of a punch he'd gotten from Neve. He rubbed it a few times and got out of bed. He had things he needed to do that day. He used the bathroom and looked at his reflection in the mirror as he brushed his teeth.

He had a bruise that was four different shades, mixing black, blue, purple, and red. He had to remember to never piss Neve off again.

He was curious to know where Bella went every day. And another part of him wanted to see his mother's lab. He knew it was somewhere in the basement of the compound. He wondered if she had ever thought of him while she was here. While he was back home alone with his grandmother going through his own nightmares.

His grandmother Alice was a woman who often lived in her own world. Addicted to mushrooms and any opioid she could get her hands on, she was barely a caregiver and was prone to violent outbursts. When she wasn't high, she would gamble what little they had with her friends Hatter, March, and Mouse. True to his name, Hatter wore an old black top hat and a white shirt with a brown vest with lots of pocket watches glued to it. He had small, brown beady eyes that always darted from side to side as though waiting for something to burst out of the shadows to attack him.

March had big ears, an overbite and pockmarks all over his skin. He was always scratching the same spot of his left cheek. He had a tan suit that was too big for him, and he kept rolling the sleeves and hem, but every time he moved, they came undone.

Mouse was incredibly short, with closely cropped black hair. His light blue eyes were bloodshot, and no matter how much coffee he drank, he was always nodding off.

They were three of the strangest people he had ever met. Things got out of hand when she ate a bad batch of mushrooms and thought the cards had come to life and were trying to kill her. That was when Jack had enough. He packed up his things and ran away. Or at least he tried to. Hatter, March, and Mouse all chased after him and dragged him back home to his grand-mother. When he finally faced her, he was sorry he'd ever set foot outside without her permission.

Jack brought himself back to the present when he spotted Bella going downstairs. She looked a little dazed, as though she hadn't slept in a while. He knew he was probably being recorded at the moment, but his curiosity was too great to ignore. Besides, he would not touch or steal anything.

He just wanted to look. No harm in that . . . right?

He followed Bella and hid behind the wall until she left the first room and went to the next room. He stepped out of his hiding place and stood in front of the door. He pulled out a small black light and held it over the keypad. It glowed bright blue and showed all of the numbers she had pushed.

1-4-8-0

He pushed the buttons hoping that was the correct combination to open the door, then let out a sigh of relief when the door opened with a soft hiss. He looked around to make sure there wasn't anyone behind him. Specifically, Neve and her steel-like fists. He rubbed his jaw remembering the injury he'd sustained yesterday.

He stepped into the room and was immediately struck by the smell of lemon cleaner and Clorox.

Someone was sleeping on the hospital bed. She had straps on her wrists and ankles.

"You must be Briar. The gardener I've heard so much about." He moved closer to the bed to inspect her. "Wow," he whispered the moment he set eyes on Briar. Even the fluorescent light couldn't diminish the golden hue of her hair. Briar's cheeks were rosy, and her lips were full and light pink. Ready to be kissed. Her skin was a little pale, but that was due to her being indoors for several weeks.

"Where is he?"

Jack jumped when heard the loud roar.

"Teddy! Don't! Nothing happened!" Bella cried.

Jack heard chains rattling and Bella screaming for help. He ran out of Briar's room and headed toward Bella's screams. He punched the code into the keypad hoping that the same number would work. Thankfully, it did. He dashed into the room as soon as the door opened.

He saw Bella with her back pressed against the wall. She had a gun pointed at someone on the other side of the room. Her hair was disheveled and her glasses were askew.

"Are you okay?" Jack took a step forward.

Bella's eyes widened in surprise as though unable to believe he was inside this room with her. "No! What are you doing here?"

Jack glanced around the room he was in. This was a stark contrast to the one Briar was sleeping in. It smelled like rotten flesh and blood. The walls were dirty and had dark handprints smeared all over them. The table was covered with papers and medical equipment and other items.

"You!" Teddy cried.

He turned around and gasped when he saw Teddy. It was a zombie that was chained to the wall. This creature was over six feet tall even hunched over. His dark blond hair was clumped and matted with blood. His red eyes were wild and filled with rage. He threw his head back and roared, showing rows of yellowed teeth.

His eyes widened in surprise and he turned to Bella. "What the fuck? A zombie? You have a fucking monster in here? Are you nuts?"

"It's a long story," Bella said.

"No shit! Come on." Jack grabbed Bella's arm and dragged her out of the lab.

"No! Mine!" Teddy cried as he reached for her, grasping only air.

"I'll come back later, Teddy," Bella promised.

The zombie roared as it tried to squeeze its arms out of its chains and chase after her. The doors closed behind them, and Jack let out a sigh of relief. Bella yanked her arm out of his grip and narrowed her eyes at him.

"Hey! Don't be mad at me. You're the one who cried for help. I helped," Jack said.

Bella looked down at the door and shook her head. "I'm sorry. You're right."

"What kind of a place are you guys running here?" Jack swiped a hand through his hair.

"Teddy is my business," she said.

He pointed at the steel door. "That thing isn't your friend. He's a monster; a beast that will rip your heart out and then munch on your brains for lunch. He's not human."

"He's my fiancé," Bella blurted.

Jack snorted and shook his head. "Is that what this whole cure thing is about? You're trying to fix him?"

Bella remained silent.

"How many years of your life have you given him?"

"It doesn't matter," she whispered.

"How long has it been?" Jack gently placed his hand over hers.

She flinched as his hands covered hers.

"Three years," she admitted.

Jack was doing his best to ignore the inhuman sounds coming from the other side of the door. "You've been watching him die," he began, "rot for three years? Wow. I hope no one ever loves me that much."

"What's that supposed to mean?"

"Not being able to let go. It's more your problem than it is his."

"You don't know what you're talking about," she said.

Jack was taken aback. "I buried my darling Mary with our unborn baby still trapped inside her. Trust me, sweetheart. I counted every shovel full of dirt. And I've counted every minute, every second I've been without her and my baby. But I'd rather know she's in heaven with our child than a fucking zombie locked in a basement."

"I won't kill him. I've tried . . . I just can't," she said between sobs.

"Do you want his suffering to end?"

Bella nodded.

"Good. I'll do it for you. Just let me know when you're ready to say goodbye."

"Thanks."

"Don't mention it."

He walked away, leaving her with the sounds of her beast-like fiancé.

FOR A WEEK STRAIGHT, JACK WENT TO SEE BRIAR BEFORE GOING outside to work on the garden. He'd sneak in after Bella left the lab, mostly because he didn't want a repeat of what had happened the last time. He didn't know why he did it. But he would sit next to Briar and tell her all about the work he had done since it was technically her garden he was tending. He told Briar about his childhood and where he'd learned how to garden. It was oddly therapeutic.

He had to keep reminding himself that she couldn't hear him since she wasn't awake. She wasn't anything like Mary, who had been shorter and had darker features. Briar was taller and had ethereal looks. As if she had been made with sunshine.

Why am I compelled to see you?

"What are you doing here?" Neve's voice shattered the silence.

Jack shouted in surprise, stumbled backwards and tipped the chair over.

He tried to think of something to say as he picked up the chair and set it down again. "Jesus H. Christ. You scared the shit out of me."

"Don't make me ask you again," Neve said.

"Nothing. I'm not some sicko that's touching an innocent woman in a coma."

"Yeah. I know. We've got cameras in here," Neve pointed at the right-hand corner of the ceiling.

He followed her finger but all he saw was a bare wall. Neve smirked. "Trust me. It's there."

"I'm surprised it took you this long to come talk to me about it. I don't care if you see me here."

"Really? Then why do you always sneak in and out of here?"

"Because my face is still recovering," he replied.

"I've given you enough time to recover. And I'm not gonna apologize because I'm not sorry I punched you. So, are you ready to talk to me?"

"Look, I followed Bella last week. I was curious."

He told her everything including Teddy's attack on Bella. But none of this information seemed to surprise Neve. She really had an eye in the sky that told her everything that was going on in the compound.

"Bella's always been the smartest woman here. Except when it comes to Teddy. Her brain turns into mush when she's anywhere near that fucking ding-dong. I think it's all because of his good looks, honestly; I always thought he was a bit of an asshole. I should've chopped his fucking head off regardless of what Bella said. But she's never asked me for anything . . . ever. So I let her play Frankenstein down here with her fiancé."

"Do you think she's close? To a cure?"

Neve chuckled.

Jack was startled to see how her face transformed. When Neve smiled, she was stunningly beautiful. It was something he knew would've made his mother insane with jealousy. And as soon as that thought crossed his mind, he brushed it aside.

"It's always the bat-shit crazy ones that find the answer, right?"

Jack sighed.

"Yeah. I feel the same way, too," she said.

Neve shook her head and placed her hands on her hips. "Just . . . keep an eye on her. If you think it has to be done, kill Teddy. I'll tell her I made you do it. Okay?"

Jack nodded and promised he would take care of it.

"Listen . . . I know it's a lot to ask. But, is it okay for me to see her? Briar?"

Neve took a moment to think before replying. "If Briar were awake, I don't think she would like it very much at first. But I like to think she'd reluctantly allow you to visit every once in a while . . . to know what's going on with her garden."

"Thanks," he said.

She put her hands up and shook her head "Not so fast, Prince Charming. Rules. Lots of them. Number one, you do not touch her. Ever. Number two, hands where we can see them. At all fucking times or I chop them off. Number three, no weird shit while you're in here. Got it?"

"Got it," he said.

He wanted to argue. To tell her he wasn't some depraved pervert or anything like that. He just wanted to talk to Briar. To see her. But he remained silent.

Neve walked out of the room and gave him another moment with Briar.

"I'll see you later, beautiful," he whispered.

Jack walked out of the room and made his way outside to the garden. He watered the soil and wondered if Briar would be able to see the garden someday. If she would wake up and smile at him.

FIFTEEN

Unable to resist, Neve returned to Zee's tower and spent the night. She woke up at dawn with Zee's arms around her waist. Neve pulled her closer to her body, loving the feeling of her smooth, warm skin against her own.

I could get used to this.

Zee patted Neve's hands and then rolled over to face her.

"It's nice to see you smile," Zee whispered.

"Oh yeah?" Neve raised an eyebrow.

"Yeah. Usually you smirk or roll your eyes. But right now? You're smiling, and it's beautiful."

Neve felt her cheeks grow warm. Before Zee had a moment to say another word and tease her about blushing, Neve pulled her in for a kiss. Zee whimpered in surprise but quickly melted into her lover's arms. Her tongue darted in and out of her mouth, causing Neve's light pink nipples to harden in response. Zee reluctantly pulled herself away. Her chest rising and falling as though she had just finished an intense workout.

"What?"

"Unless you're planning on spending the day here, you'd better get going. If you don't, I'm gonna tie you to this bed and pleasure you until you are limp," Zee said.

"Is that a promise?" Neve grinned.

"I know you have a lot to do today. You'll be mad if it doesn't get done."

Neve threw herself back onto the bed and groaned. Zee was right.

"This wouldn't be an issue if you asked your friends to help you every once in a while," Zee said.

"I know. I've been meaning ask Gus to do a bit more around the compound," Neve said.

"That's the spirit," Zee teased.

"What are you going to do today?" Neve climbed out of the warm bed she was already missing.

"Oh. The usual," Zee replied as the sheets slid off her body, revealing her small breasts.

Neve was tempted to touch them before leaving, but she knew if she did, she would never make it out the door. Instead, she turned her gaze away and looked for her clothes. "Which is?"

"Keep an eye on everyone and make sure no zombies sneak up on us. I might tidy up in here, now that I have company more often," Zee said.

Neve slipped her long sleeve, navy-blue T-shirt over her head and slid her khaki cargo pants on. She reached for her belt. "I hope that's not a problem. My being here."

"Are you kidding? I never thought it would happen. Half the time you're here I think I'm hallucinating the whole thing," Zee admitted.

"That good, huh?" Neve said.

"Stop." Zee threw a pillow at her.

Neve caught the pillow midair and tossed it back onto the bed. "And now you're the one blushing."

Zee giggled before sticking out her tongue. She threw some clothes on and walked over to her desk, then flopped on her chair and typed a few things on the keyboard. Zee stared at the monitors in front of her for a few moments quickly checking the grounds of The Orchard making sure they were all safe for another night.

While she pulled on her boots, Neve said, "Is he still going down to see her? Even after we had our little chat?"

"Yep," Zee replied. She spun around in her desk chair and let out a wistful sigh.

"What?"

Zee shrugged as she slowly spun in the opposite direction to untangle her long hair from the bottom of the chair. "I dunno. It's just . . . it's kinda sweet. Jack sits and talks to her for an hour and then leaves."

"Does he touch her?"

"Nope. He sits next to her and clasps his hands together, almost like he's praying or something."

Neve wrinkled her nose. "Weird."

"If I were in a coma, would you visit me every day?"

"Of course I would. And then I would hunt down whoever or whatever hurt you and rip its spine out its body." Neve kissed her on the top of the head and silently prayed that nothing ever happened to Zee.

"Awww. You're so sweet. I love you," Zee said charmingly, as if Neve had offered to pick up a pint of ice cream instead of threatening to murder anything that dared harm her.

"I love you, too." She sighed, pressed her forehead against Zee's, and closed her eyes. Neve reluctantly pulled herself away from her girlfriend. "All right, I'm gonna go do my rounds, bark a little bit at people, and tinker with my droids."

"Okay."

"You want me to stay tonight?"

Zee gave her a mischievous grin. "Yes, please."

"Any special requests?"

"Do we still have ramen noodles in the basement? Or are they all gone?"

"Yeah, we still have a few cases left."

"Can you bring me some? If you have any of the lime shrimp ones left, bring them all to me please. Those are my favorite."

Neve smiled. "Sure thing. I'll see you later."

"Bye."

Neve reluctantly walked out of Zee's apartment. The moment she stood out in the hallway, she immediately felt the difference.

It was colder . . .

Neve ran her hands over her arms to warm herself a bit and headed downstairs to go back to work. The compound was a well-oiled machine, but it took a lot of work for it to stay that way.

She thought about the things that had been happening in their compound over the past few weeks and how it was connected to Lila. She knew she would face her soon. Neve wasn't sure she was ready. Would she be able to kill her and avenge her father? Or had love made her soft? Would Neve be able to forgive her for what she had done? For plunging the whole world into chaos, death, and decay?

By the time she made it outside, she wasn't so sure.

JACK SNUCK BACK INTO BRIAR'S ROOM. HIS BREATH CAUGHT IN HIS chest every time he looked at her. She was unnaturally beautiful. The high cheekbones. The soft pink lips. The way her golden blond hair fell into soft waves. The slow yet gentle rise and fall of her chest. He longed to caress her skin and kiss her lips. But he knew he was being watched. Every move he made was carefully recorded and studied.

Even though Neve was intense, he was still happy to be here. She was just trying to protect her friends and home. He didn't blame her at all, especially now that she knew who his mother was. He knew one false move would get him kicked out. He'd be back to scavenging for food and sleeping on treetops and in dilapidated houses, one of the few reminders that a far different life had once existed in this world.

Jack remembered what Neve said about the attack not too far from the compound. He couldn't help but think of the similarities between what was happening now and what had happened with his old friends. Part of him wanted to pick up his shit and leave. But another side of him wanted to stay with Briar until the very end. To be the brave prince who fought the evil dragon and kept it away from the beautiful sleeping damsel.

Could I do it? Could I sacrifice it all for a woman I've never even spoken to, at least not while she's awake?

"Briar? Can you hear me?" Jack whispered.

He rested his chin on the edge of the bed and watched her sleep.

"You should know . . . I'm a coward," he whispered. "I'm not the guy who will save the day. I'm the asshole piece of shit who'll leave you to die. I'll be the one who disappears in the middle of the night while his friends beg and fight for their lives."

He picked up a lock of Briar's hair and twirled it between his fingers. That was the only time he dared to touch her. He brought it to his lips and kissed it. Jack caught a whiff of citrus that lingered even after he stood, ready to leave the room.

"I'm sorry," he whispered. "I shouldn't have done that." But she had cast a spell on him.

He made his way toward the door when he noticed something out of the corner of his eye: a jagged L.B. on the wall, slightly covered by a tall filing cabinet.

His mother's initials. They had to be.

L.B.

Lila Beauchamp.

It had to be her.

He pushed the filing cabinet out of the way and saw the initials clearly. He frowned and wondered why she had carved her initials on the wall. He ran his hand over the wall to see if there was anything hidden there and discovered a different texture from one part of the wall to the other. One part was much smoother, and another was rough like brick. He pulled his

Swiss army knife from his back pocket and used the small blade to scrape the paint off part of the wall, revealing a metal panel.

He looked around to make sure Neve wasn't lurking somewhere behind him. He was alone. Jack slowly opened the panel. He wondered what could be hidden behind the wall. A note? A vial with a cure? He shook his head. His mother wasn't that generous. He pulled his hand away, afraid of what he would find on the other side. Perhaps ignorance was bliss.

But he had come all this way . . . he had to know.

He hadn't confessed the entire truth to Neve. He'd purposely sought out The Orchard to find out what his mother had been doing here. He *needed* to know. Pushing his hesitation away, he reached into the hidden space. His fingers touched something pushed far back that felt like a book. He pulled his hand back out and stared at the old-fashioned notebook, knowing immediately it had been his mothers. Flipping through it he found that it was filled with notes and observations that Lila had made on her experiments.

"Oh my God," he whispered. With this information, there was a real chance that they could reverse it or even find a cure.

ZEE SIGHED AND TURNED HER ATTENTION BACK TO JACK. SHE COULDN'T hear what he said, but he had walked away from Briar's side and found something in the lab. Zee tried to zoom in and get a closer look, but it was far too dark. They would have to send someone to go fix the lights in that room. She turned on her communicator and called her girlfriend.

"Neve, are you there?" Zee said.

"Yeah. I'm here. What is it?" Neve said.

"Jack," Zee said.

"Where is he?" Neve asked.

"Where do you think?"

"Visiting Sleeping Beauty."

"Is that what we're calling her now? Should I be worried?" Zee whispered.

"You're cute when you're jealous," Neve teased.

Zee rolled her eyes. "Who said anything about jealous?" She quickly pinpointed Neve's location in the compound.

She was in the kitchen. There was an old monitor that Zee had access to. "I'm going to patch this feed over to you so you can see it."

"Okay."

Zee looked at the monitor and saw that Jack was visiting Briar in what once was Lila's old laboratory. Neve had gotten rid of the majority of her things, but Zee often wondered if she had missed anything. Her eyes widened in surprise when she saw that the filing cabinet had been pushed out of the way.

"Zoom in," Neve said.

"Okay," Zee replied. With a few keystrokes, she could zoom in on the camera.

Zee peered at the screen, and even though it was dark in that part of the room, she made out a couple of letters. L and B.

"Fucking bitch!" Neve cried.

"What?" Zee asked.

"Lila hid something behind the filing cabinet. It never occurred to me to check for something like that," Neve said.

"You were a grief-stricken kid. It's okay. You did the best you could," Zee said, doing her best to soothe her lover.

Neve shook her head. "My father deserved better than that. This place is all I have left of him."

"Looks like he found an old notebook," Zee said.

"Keep an eye on him," Neve said. "I'm gonna see what's in that notebook."

SIXTEEN

"No, no, no, no . . ." Jack muttered as he continued to read through the notebook.

He had been thirteen when his mother vanished in the middle of the night, leaving him alone with his grandmother.

"Where is Momma?" a teenage Jack had asked the next morning.

Alice pointed a crooked finger at him. "You do not get to ask such questions. Your mother is exactly where she is meant to be. Now be quiet and eat your breakfast."

Jack picked up his spoon and ate his oatmeal. He knew better than to cross his grandmother. He counted the days until his mother returned. He didn't understand what was going on, but he kept his head down and stayed out of Alice's way.

Then almost three years to the day, Lila and Michael returned. He hadn't seen Michael since before his mother had left. He'd been a constant presence for years but then one day, he'd vanished. Jack had suspected that Michael and his mother had been having an affair and Michael had grown tired of Lila, leaving her. Now he was back but where had he been all these years?

His mother had gained a little weight, and she looked exhausted. She was paler than he remembered. Her blue eyes were muted, lifeless, as if every little bit of joy had been sucked out of her soul.

He went up to his mother and welcomed her home. He leaned forward to give her a hug, but she patted him on the shoulder and walked past him as though he were nothing.

"Mom?" Jack whispered.

"Leave her alone," Michael whispered.

"But . . ."

"But nothing," Michael said. He shoved Jack out of the way and followed Lila as she made her way to her room.

Jack glared at them as they walked away from him.

That night he overheard them talking when they thought he was asleep.

"You stayed longer than you said you would," Grandma Alice said.

"I know. I'm sorry. It took longer than I thought it would to get him to trust me," Lila said.

"She married him," Michael said and then took a swig of his beer.

"You did what?" Alice shrieked.

"Shh. You'll wake him up. And yes, I married him. It was the only way to gain access to his orchard," Lila said.

"Really?"

"Yeah. Like I said, he had trust issues," Lila said.

"And he let you get away?" Grandma asked.

"No," Lila whispered.

"Charles is dead," Michael said.

Grandma Alice shook her head. "Is this a mess we have to go back to clean up?"

"I had no choice," Lila had said. "He kept asking me too many questions. He couldn't know the apples in his orchard were special. The acidity in the apples is perfect for what I have in mind. And no . . . leave them alone. At least for now."

Jack's hands shook as the memory faded, the notebook still in his grip. He remembered the apple Neve had given him the day he arrived at the compound. The apples. That's why his mother had left him. He was yet another victim in her pursuit of beauty. He knew what she'd done. Knew of the initial experiments in the basement of his grandmother's home. The failed experiments that had created the virus. The mess his grandmother had needed to clean up, but they hadn't been careful enough and the virus had mutated once the initial victims died. The rest was history.

And for what? All of it for beauty. He would have loved her no matter what she'd looked like. To him, his mother had been the most beautiful woman in the world. Until the day she'd tossed him aside like the virus ridden zombies she'd created.

"I have to get out of here," he muttered, realizing what Neve would think if she discovered him with the notebook.

He shoved the notebook in his back pocket and was about to walk out the door when suddenly, he froze.

Briar.

Even in her sleep, she had power over him that was overwhelming. He couldn't leave without saying goodbye. Jack knew he was wasting time. He knew he would probably get caught for slowing down for even a second, but he went back inside, determined to give his 'sleeping beauty' a proper farewell.

"I wish I had gotten a chance to meet you for real. Take you on a date and tell you some lame joke just to make you smile. But maybe in another life we'll get it right. Goodbye," he whispered.

Jack took a deep and steadying breath, leaned in, and kissed Briar on the lips. Warmth radiated from her. Briar's skin was as soft as a rose petal.

Perfect.

That was the only word Jack could think of at that particular moment. He stepped away from her, ready to leave when he noticed Briar frowning. Her eyes fluttered open, startling him with their deep blue color.

Briar's eyes locked with his, and she gasped in surprise. She tried to put her hands up, but they were still strapped down.

"Who the fuck are you?" Briar shouted.

"I'm Jack," he replied.

Briar narrowed her eyes and then arched her left eyebrow. "Yeah . . . that's super fucking helpful. Where the hell is Neve?"

"I–I–I'm a friend of hers. I just moved here," he stammered.

"I don't give a fuck. Now get me out of here," Briar said.

"Ummm . . . I dunno," he muttered.

"If you don't untie me right now," Briar growled, "I will make your life a fucking nightmare when I do get out of here."

"Oh, okay," Jack said as he undid the straps on her wrists and ankles.

Briar glared at him. "Did you do anything weird to me while I was asleep? If I find out that you did some fucked up stuff to me, I'll kick the living shit out of you. Got it?"

Jack nodded so fast he thought his head would pop off his shoulders. When her hands were finally free, Briar reached out and grabbed Jack's shirt. With surprising strength, especially for someone who had been in a coma for several weeks, she pulled him to her. Briar's breath smelled like sewage, but he sure as hell wasn't going to tell her that.

"Go. Get. Neve. Now!" Briar growled. "Okay."

Briar shoved him away, and he ran out the door as quickly as possible. He bumped into Bella on his way out the door.

"Hey! Briar's awake," Jack said.

Bella looked at the door and then back at Jack. "What? How?"

"I'll tell you later. I gotta go find Neve. Any idea where she is?"

"No idea. I'll call her, hang on."

Bella used her communicator and called Neve. Some static came through and then Neve's voice came in loud and clear. "Neve here."

"Briar's awake. She wants to see you."

"I'm on my way," Neve replied.

"Okay. At least I saved you from going on a wild goose chase. Now tell me. What happened? More importantly . . . what did you do?" Bella crossed her arms over her chest and stared at Jack.

Even though he was tempted, Jack knew better than to lie. They had cameras everywhere, and the truth would come out eventually.

"I kissed her, and she woke up."

"You what?" Bella shrieked.

Jack groaned, and he felt his cheeks grow warm. "I know. It was a stupid impulsive thing to do. But look on the bright side. She woke up."

Bella rolled her eyes and groaned. "Such a guy thing to do. See a body in the middle of the woods, and you can't just leave it alone. You have to kiss it, fuck it, or poke it with a stick."

"I'm sorry."

"You're lucky Briar's too weak to rip your face off. I would run and hide if I were you. Because once she's feeling one hundred percent better, she's coming after you. And it won't be pretty."

"And umm . . . she's also in serious need of a toothbrush. Her breath is really bad," Jack whispered.

Bella's lips twitched as though she were trying hard not to smile.

Together, they went to Briar's room. Her eyes lit up with joy when she saw Bella, but her smile faded when she saw Jack as though suspicious of him. He didn't blame her; he was a stranger after all.

"Hey, Briar," Bella said. "How do you feel?"

"Bella! Thank God you're here. What the hell happened to me? And who the fuck is this guy?" Briar pointed an accusatory finger at Jack.

"You've been in a coma for several weeks," Bella began her explanation. "Your body has been fighting the infection that snake passed on to you. And this is Jack. He's been here for a couple of weeks, and he's been taking care of your garden."

Briar gave him a suspicious look but didn't say anything. Jack gave her a warm smile and did his best to seem approachable. He wanted her to like him or at least stop shooting daggers at him with her cerulean eyes.

"How's my garden?" Briar whispered.

Jack perked up, happy that she was asking him a question. "Good. Thriving now that I'm using a different compost. Starting to get little tomatoes and strawberries again. It'll be a while before they're ready to be picked though."

He was relieved to be able to talk to her about something she cared about. "Good."

Bella sighed and talked about the studies she'd made on Briar while she was sleeping. She used a lot of words Jack didn't understand, and after a while it all sounded like white noise to him. All he saw was Briar.

"I want to run some more tests on you so I'll need you down here with me every day."

"Ugh. Fine. Can I get out of here?"

"Can you move your legs?" Bella inquired.

"Sorta, kinda," Briar replied.

"Do you want Jack to take you to your room? We have an old wheelchair around here somewhere. It creaks a bit, but it'll get you to your room. We'll get you something to eat and drink, too."

Briar nodded. "Yes, please. I'm starving. I could eat a freakin' elephant."

"We'll start you on some broth and then slowly work your way to some solids," Bella said.

"Ugh," Briar said.

"Jack, do you mind standing outside and waiting for Neve? We need some privacy," Bella said.

"Yeah, sure. No problem." Jack averted his eyes. He wanted to make sure he made a good impression on Briar from this moment forward. The door opened, and he stepped out into the hallway where Neve was already waiting for him. His heart almost burst out of his chest when he saw the way she looked at him. Like she wanted to rip his balls off and shove them down his throat.

"That's not a good look," he mumbled.

"Care to explain yourself?" Neve glared.

"Ummm . . ."

"Ummm is not an answer. It's something morons say when they're hiding something. Zee and I saw you in Briar's room. Show me what you found." Neve stuck her hand out and waited.

Jack was confused for a moment. What was she talking about? Then it dawned on him. Neve wasn't mad about him kissing Briar. She knew he had his mother's notebook rolled up in his back pocket.

"You don't wanna see what's in that notebook," Jack said.

Neve punched the wall behind him, cracking some of the bricks, causing parts of the wall to crumble and fall to the floor.

"I'll decide what I can and cannot see. Now hand it over. Or the next time I throw a punch, it'll be on your fucking face. Maybe I'll bruise the other side of your jaw so your face is even."

"Neve . . ."

"May I remind you that you are standing in my property. So anything you find in that room or anywhere in this compound already belongs to me. Nothing in this compound is yours. Are we clear? Nothing is Lila's or yours. Every day that bitch was here was a goddamned gift from my father. So hand it over."

"Yes, ma'am." Jack took a deep breath and handed Lila's notebook over to Neve. She snatched the notebook from Jack's hand and read it. The more she read, the deeper her frown became until her eyebrows were almost touching each other.

"Why would you want to keep this from me? Why would you want to take it? What's it to you?"

"I was curious. I wanted to read more before I decided what to do with it," Jack said.

"Why not give it to Bella? At least she would know what to do with this kind of information."

Jack shrugged. He didn't know what to say to that. He had wanted something to belong to him and him alone for a moment. Something that could connect him to his mother. To see if she had mentioned him somewhere in her notes. He doubted it, but he had wanted to see for himself.

Neve rolled up the notebook and sighed. "Talk to me, Jack. What's really going on here?"

Jack opened his mouth to speak but was interrupted by Bella.

"You can come back inside now," she said.

"Okay," he said. Jack took a step towards the door, thinking he was free of his confession with Neve.

She let out a sharp whistle, forcing him to turn toward the sound. "We're not done here. Talk," Neve said.

Jack nodded.

"Why did Lila want to marry my father? Out of every compound in the world, out of every single man in the world why him? Why?" Neve asked.

"I think it has something to do with the apples," Jack said.

"Apples?"

He took the apple seeds from his pocket, holding them as if they were the greatest treasure in the universe.

"I don't know what you know about what's happening outside this place. This . . . oasis you've created, but the country has turned into absolute shit. The little food you've been able to grow here is a miracle. This is the only place apples exist. They don't grow anywhere else. At least not since the virus ravaged most of the world. The only reason I knew what it was is because I saw a picture of it in a book when I was a little kid. Just look for yourself."

He reached out and gently grabbed the notebook from Neve's hands. Curious, she allowed it. He unrolled the notebook and looked through Lila's notes until found the passage he was looking for.

"There. See?" He pointed at the page and passed the notebook to Neve. She read it.

I have finally earned an apple from Charles. I've never seen anything like it. The flavor is indescribable. I understand why Charles doesn't allow anyone to enter the orchard. It is a hallowed place. This is a very special fruit and must be tended to with the utmost care. I've run many tests on this one fruit, and I see that the answer to my dilemma is in this apple. The acidity is just right. A few minor adjustments to the pH levels, and it should be perfect. The seeds of these apples contain small amounts of amygdalin, a sugar and cyanide compound known as a cyanogenic glycoside. Ingesting small amounts of apple seeds will cause no ill effects but in extremely large doses can cause adverse reactions. It may take several hours before the poison takes effect as cyanogenic glycosides must be hydrolyzed before the cyanide ion is released. But I can take those ingredients and do just about anything. I can make a poison. I can create a potion to keep me young forever. I could even use it to reverse the effects of the Aetervia virus. My greatest creation and curse.

All I have to do is produce enough of them to take home with me. As much as I've come to care for Charles, this isn't my home. I don't belong here. The ghost of his wife Violet haunts these walls. I see her everywhere, especially in Neve's eyes.

I'm only going to stay here long enough to figure out why the apples grow here and here alone. Apples. Who knew? I love the color, ruby red. I wish I had lips that deep red.

Neve let the notebook slip off her fingers and fall on the floor between her feet with a loud slap. That was why Lila was at the compound. The apples. Charles was the only one who had access to the small orchard in the back of their home. They were the only ones with the codes needed to get past the steel doors. Charles always shared the apples with everyone in the compound, but he didn't want everyone in his quiet place. It was where he went to think, meditate, and be alone. And ever since his passing, Neve was the only one with the codes.

Seems like a valid reason to marry a guy, Neve thought sarcastically. *Just stick around long enough to see if he'll share his favorite spot and see where it takes you.*

"But how did she know about the apples in the first place?" Neve murmured.

Jack shrugged. "I think Michael had something to do with it. He followed her around like a lap dog back home. He must've found out about this place and told Lila. That's how she ended up here."

Neve nodded. That made sense. He could've found a way to get information to someone outside of the compound. This was back when they had plenty of fuel, and Michael had easy access to the truck.

Neve studied Jack for a moment, feeling like there was something he wasn't telling her. Something nudged at her. "Jack, did Lila and Michael really meet here?"

He looked startled, a reaction that confirmed her suspicion. "No," he said hesitantly. "Michael lived with us for a few years and then he disappeared. I always wondered why and where he'd gone but now, I know he came here."

Neve was shocked. So, Michael hadn't come to The Orchard on his own initiative. His friendship with her father had been a farce, another strand to the web of lies Lila had sewn. She had sent him here to gain her father's trust and to give her a way into their life.

"I'm sorry, Neve. She's a manipulator. Michael got what he deserved. He played into her hands and paid the ultimate price."

"My father paid the price, too." She reached down and picked up the notebook she'd dropped. The final piece to the puzzle she'd been trying to work since the day Charles had died and Lila had left the compound.

Jack gave her a sad smile. "We all did."

She nodded and gripped the notebook tightly. "Looks like I have some reading to do."

Jack took a step toward Briar's room, but Neve grabbed him by the arm and pulled him back.

"Unh unh. Not so fast, Prince Charming. You stay away from Briar."

"But . . . I didn't do anything to hurt her," he said.

"I don't care. She doesn't know who you are. Give her space," Neve said.

Jack glanced back at the door with longing and nodded.

"I'll tell her what happened. But if you find anything else that you think belonged to Lila, hand it over to me or Bella. No questions asked. Understand?"

"Yeah," he whispered.

Jack parted his lips as though wanting to say something else, but he closed his lips and remained silent instead.

"What?"

"Did Michael have a room here?"

"Of course he did. He was my father's right-hand man."

"You should probably check it out. See if he had anything hidden in there. Maybe he had a connection to other compounds."

"I'd have to check the old records and see which room was his. I can't remember. It's been nine years since everything happened. But . . . thanks for the suggestion."

Jack nodded before turning to leave.

Neve held the notebook tightly in her hands. She wasn't sure how she would contain the turbulent thoughts and emotions that threatened to overtake her.

SEVENTEEN

BRIAR SPENT THE NIGHT IN THE SAME STERILE ROOM THAT BELLA and Neve had put her in. She woke up at what she could only assume was the crack of dawn, it was hard to tell since there were no windows and the clock was on the wall behind her. She distracted herself by trying to wiggle her toes and force her body out of atrophy. She would walk again even if it killed her, which she was almost certain it would. She remembered little about what happened the day she got bitten. The entire episode was a blur for her.

She did remember the dreams she had while she slept. They were quite vivid and terrifying. She was too scared to close her eyes for fear she would fall into the dream world once more. In her dreams, she was a princess in a long, ivory gown forced to hide in the forest because a powerful fairy had placed a curse on her. Briar wandered in the forest until she found a haunted castle.

It was a tall, dark, and imposing building. She studied the walls and saw they had been painted with hot, sticky tar. But no matter how hard she tried to run away from it, all paths led to this strange castle. Eventually, she went inside.

She found an old spinning wheel, and even though she knew it would hurt her, she plunged her index finger on the needle of the spinning wheel.

She fell on the floor with a heavy thud and fell asleep. The fairy turned into a large black dragon that guarded the castle and kept everyone outside and away from her.

Everyone . . . except one person. A tall, blonde man with sad, haunted eyes. She had no idea who he was, but he was the only one willing to face the dragon to save her.

All Briar wanted was to go outside and feel the warm sunshine against her skin. But instead of sending Briar back to her room, Bella changed had her mind and kept her in the lab because she wanted to run a few more tests. Briar hated this bed, the plain white color and the smell of the room. She wanted to go to her bedroom. It was painted pale green with little pink rosettes along the edges. And her bed, while small, had pink bed sheets and smelled like clean soap.

She tried to stand up on her own, but her limbs were still too weak. That burst of energy she'd had when she woke up must've been a fluke. She wished she could conjure that strength once more. She hated not being able to move freely.

This was hell.

Her heart jumped when she heard the door slide open.

Bella walked through the door wearing her white lab coat and carrying a chart in her hands. "Morning, Briar. How are you today?"

"Hungry."

Bella gave her a worried look. "For?"

Briar gave her a scathing glare. "Food."

"What kind of food?"

"A fucking pancake would be nice. Or at least some fucking crackers. Jesus Christ, Bella. I'm not a zombie. I didn't turn. I'm pale as fuck, but I'm not ashy, and I sure hope my eyes haven't changed colors."

Bella sighed with relief and tucked a loose strand of hair behind her ear.

"I'm not a zombie," Briar whispered. She grabbed the pillow behind her and held it against her chest.

"I know, but it's my job to check up on you and ask these questions. We still don't know how this happened. And there's no way of knowing if something will change now that you're finally awake. I know this sucks, but everything I'm doing is to protect you and everyone here."

"I know. But still." Briar pouted.

"I'll have some food sent to you as soon as possible," Bella promised.

"Good. I'm starving. That broth you gave me yesterday did absolutely nothing for my appetite."

Bella chuckled. Briar was never shy about food or her love of pancakes. "So far your bloodwork looks clear. There aren't any traces of the virus in you. But I would like to check your blood regularly at least for the next couple of weeks."

Briar nodded.

"Can I go to my room now? I can eat my breakfast there. This room is creepy as fuck."

"Just one more test, and if you stay for a few more minutes, then I can have you sent to your room," Bella said.

"Okay."

Bella put on a pair of lavender latex-free gloves and carefully searched for a vein in Briar's arm. She wiped the skin clean with antiseptic, then with expert precision, she inserted the needle and drew some of Briar's blood. Once that was finished, she placed a bandage on her arm.

"So, what do you think about Jack?" Bella asked as she placed the blood sample on her desk.

Briar shrugged. "He's cute. But too skinny."

Bella sat at the desk and typed her notes onto the computer. "That's probably because he was basically starving until he arrived. He's been here for a few weeks . . . I think? Geez, time is a blur right now. Anyway, he's been coming here every morning just to talk to you. It was cute watching him sneak in and out of here even though he knew we were watching him closely."

"Seriously?"

"Yep," Bella replied.

"Huh."

"Yeah. I've never seen anyone so smitten. Good thing he never heard you talk. It might've taken him a lot longer to approach you." Bella laughed as she continued to type.

"What's he like?" Briar asked.

Bella shrugged. "He seems nice. A little reserved. I'm sure he's still hiding something that will piss off Neve if she finds out what it is. But if you push him enough, I think he'd tell you what you wanna know. He's still figuring out how to live here with us."

"Okay. Why isn't he here?"

"Neve told him to give you space. She wasn't sure how scared and pissed off you were, so she told him to back off."

Briar picked at the invisible lint on the corner of her pillow and nodded. "Yeah, that makes sense."

Bella gave her a sly grin. "You want me to ask him to come back? I can talk to Neve if you want."

Briar thought about it for a moment. Remembering the man she saw in her dream. She nodded and said, "I guess, I mean, he spent all that time with me. It wouldn't hurt to talk to him at least."

"You're not mad he kissed you?" Bella asked as she spun around in her chair and faced her friend.

Briar fidgeted with her fingers, picking at her cuticles and marveling over how clean they were. There was a faint scar on her index and middle finger where the snake had bitten her. She was thankful that Bella had taken such meticulous care of her while she was asleep. But she missed seeing little bits of dirt caked under her nails and in her fingerprints. "I mean ... it was fucking weird that he did that. But it woke me up so that's a good thing. Right?"

"I haven't been kissed in three years. Any action I can get is welcome," Bella said.

Briar giggled.

"Laugh it up," Bella said in a dry tone.

"Sorry. All right, tell him to get his skinny ass here and help me get some food."

Bella nodded.

"So, what's the verdict on the whole blood test thing?" Briar nodded toward the computer.

"So far, so good. Whatever that snake injected into your body was very faint. You're lucky you didn't turn. It's almost as if your body shut itself down to fight the virus."

"Weird."

"No. Not weird. Miraculous. There is a chance your blood cells have certain antibodies that could be the key to a cure. If it's okay with you, I'd like your permission to study your blood."

"Do you need to take more of my blood?"

Bella shook her head. "No. I have everything I need with what I have right now."

"Sounds good. Can I get the fuck outta here now, please?"

Bella grinned. "Awww. You said please. How sweet. I missed you."

"Sure you have. Now get that skinny motherfucker in here and tell him I want a giant stack of pancakes. Please and thank you."

Bella used her communicator and called Jack's room. He still hadn't gotten his own communicator. There was no response in his room, so Bella tried the garden and lucked out.

Briar strained her hearing to see if she could hear his side of the conversation, but all she got were muddled words.

"Hey, Jack. I could use a hand with Briar . . . Yeah. She needs someone to take her to the kitchen and make her breakfast . . . No, you don't have to carry her. I have a wheelchair here you can use . . . Awesome. Thank you." Bella laughed. "No . . . Don't worry. I'll talk to Neve. I promise you won't get in trouble." She turned back to Briar. "He's on his way."

"Do you have a hairbrush here?" Briar lightly tugged her fingers through her knotted hair.

Bella smirked. "Yeah, and a toothbrush, too."

Briar checked her breath and gasped in horror. "Oh God. Ewww."

"Yeah. I can smell it all the way over here."

"God. What the fuck? Why didn't you tell me sooner? You think you know a person."

Together they got Briar to look presentable for Jack. She still wasn't sure how she felt about him. But she wanted to give him a chance. At some point, she needed to ask Zee to let her watch the videos of him in her room. She wanted to know what he'd said while she'd slept. *What had he confessed to her?*

There was a soft knock on the door. Briar gasped softly and waited for Bella to answer it. The door slid open and there was Jack. Still too thin, but his blue eyes looked hopeful when they met Briar's. He gave her an awkward smile and then quickly averted his eyes. His clothes were dirty and his shoes were caked with dirt. She took a deep breath taking in the smell of grass, dirt, and sunshine. God, she couldn't wait to go back outside.

"Good morning," he said.

"Morning," Bella said.

"I'm here just as you asked."

"Thank you. If you can please take Briar upstairs and get her something to eat, that would be great."

"Sure thing. Morning, Briar." Jack glanced over at her then, blushing, he looked down at the floor.

"Morning," Briar said.

"So . . . wheelchair?" Jack looked around.

"It's right there," Bella said and pointed to the folded wheelchair on the other side of the room.

Jack grabbed the blue wheelchair, unfolded it, and pushed it next to Briar's bed. In one swift move, he scooped her up in his arms.

Briar let out a whoop of delight that quickly turned in a fit of giggles as she clung to Jack. He gave her a bashful grin as he carefully placed her onto the wheelchair.

"Thanks," she whispered.

"You're welcome."

"See you later," Bella said.

"Bye," Briar said.

Jack and Briar didn't say much to each other as he pushed her wheelchair down the hallway and into the elevator. He took her to the kitchen and got started with her breakfast. He busied himself by making her eggs and pancakes. She breathed in the delicious smell of food. Her stomach groaned in protest, making its presence known.

"Sorry," she whispered, bashfully covering her belly.

"It's okay. The eggs should be ready in a few minutes. We'll get you started with that, and then I'll make you a small pancake," he said as he flipped the pancake. On the other frying pan, he scrambled the eggs, making them nice and fluffy.

Briar grinned and shook her head in disbelief. "A guy cooking for me. I never thought I'd see the day," she said.

"Don't get too excited. This is all I can do. Just simple and basic stuff."

"Simple is good," Briar replied.

"Here we go. Breakfast is served." He placed a plate of scrambled eggs in front of her, then a perfectly golden pancake with a small square of yellow butter in the middle. There was a small jar of maple syrup on the table ready to be poured over it.

"Oops. I forgot the utensils. Hang on." Jack found a fork and placed it next to her hand.

"This looks amazing. Thank you," Briar said.

Her hand trembled as she reached for the fork. She decided to start small and work her way to more food. She took a tiny bite of the scrambled eggs and let out a loud moan.

"So good," she murmured.

Briar ate it within seconds. She grabbed the syrup and poured it over her pancake. She loved pancakes. Fluffy, sweet and gooey goodness. They didn't make them often, so this was a special treat. She cut up a small piece and closed her eyes as she chewed it.

"Oh God. I missed this so much," she said between bites.

Jack cleared his throat. "Do you want some coffee?"

She shook her head. "No thanks. I don't drink coffee."

"Tea? Water?"

"Tea would be nice."

Jack got up, and she averted her eyes when he adjusted his pants.

"This is amazing. Thank you so much," Briar said between bites.

"You're welcome and make sure you pace yourself. You don't wanna eat too fast," he warned.

"Oh God. I don't care. I just want it all in my mouth."

He put a mug of water in the microwave and set it for one minute and thirty seconds. While that was heating up, he sat next to her and sipped his coffee.

She sat back and took a deep breath. She patted her stomach and reveled in the fact that she was full to burst. Briar knew she shouldn't have eaten so much. There was a slight chance that she would throw it all up, but she didn't care.

"Can I ask you something?" Briar swirled her finger in the leftover syrup on her plate.

"Yeah."

She brought her syrup covered finger to her lips and licked it clean.

"Why did you kiss me?"

Jack groaned. He covered his eyes with his left hand and shook his head.

She wasn't sure if it was from embarrassment or what she just did with the syrup.

"I'm not pissed off anymore. I mean it's what finally woke my ass up, so thanks for that. I was just curious."

He lowered his hand and looked into her eyes. "I was thinking about leaving the compound. I was saying goodbye to you in case I followed through," he admitted.

"Really? Why?"

He was saved by the microwave beeping. He got up, took the mug out of the microwave, and placed a tea bag in the hot water. He placed it in front of Briar and sighed. "I panicked. Zombies are attacking this area, and it's what happened to me the last time. Plus, I'm not good around people. Which is why you were so easy to talk to, you didn't talk back."

"At least you're honest. I'd rather have someone tell the truth than feed me a bunch of bullshit," Briar said.

Jack chuckled.

"What?"

"I never expected someone so beautiful to curse so much."

Briar rolled her eyes. "Yeah. I get that all the time."

BELLA LOOKED AT A RECENT SAMPLE OF BRIAR'S BLOOD THROUGH the microscope. She immediately noticed that there were more white blood cells and they were . . . bigger.

"What the hell?" Bella muttered.

She studied the cells and watched as they interacted with each other on the dish. She zoomed in and then furrowed her brows.

"Hmm, I wonder . . ." Bella whispered.

She added a small droplet of Teddy's blood into Briar's sample and looked into the microscope once more. Teddy's blue-black blood cells swirled around Briar's healthy blood cells. His cells looked ready to devour Briar's cells. Bella's jaw dropped when she saw Briar's white blood cells destroy the virus within Teddy's blood. Leaving his red and white blood cells completely unharmed.

"Oh my God!" Bella pushed her chair away from her desk and covered her lips. "Oh. My. God!"

She did the same thing a few times with different samples just to verify her findings, and they all had the exact result.

Briar's blood was the cure she had been searching for. With this, she could create a cure and maybe a vaccine.

She gathered all of the necessary ingredients: sterile water, albumin, phenols, and glycine. Some adjuvants to help improve the vaccine's effectiveness, and for several hours, Bella took a quarter of Briar's blood sample and created a vaccine. She had several variations of the cure because she wasn't sure which of the ingredients would react well with Briar's blood sample. Once she had that ready, she placed it in the dart gun to shoot at Teddy from a safe distance. With everything she needed on hand, she headed into Teddy's room next door.

"What . . . doing?" Teddy groaned when he saw Bella.

"Trying something new," she replied as she placed everything on the table.

"Kill me . . ." he muttered as he covered his face with his hands.

"If this doesn't work, I promise you I'll chop your head off myself," she said. Teddy sighed in response.

Bella closed her eyes for a moment. She knew how he felt, or at least she tried to empathize with him. She was tired of living like this, too. Hopefully, she had the answer to all their problems in her hands.

"Here goes nothin'," she whispered.

She took a deep breath and fired. The dart flew with a soft whistle and landed right above Teddy's heart. He grunted but remained silent as if she wasn't there.

Bella sat on the chair and waited. She watched patiently over her dead fiancé and hoped that it would work. She swore to herself that this would be her last attempt at a cure. She would let him go if this didn't work. She would find a way to finally move on.

She sat and took notes for several hours ignoring her groaning stomach.

It yawned with hunger she couldn't keep at bay. Bella was ready to call it a day when she heard Teddy moan and growl.

"Teddy? Talk to me, baby. Are you okay?" she asked.

"Dunno," he slurred. "Feel . . . strange." Teddy got up. He lost his balance and fell down. Bella had to stop herself from rushing to his side. There was no way of knowing what would happen to Teddy. So she stood still and waited.

"Come into the light. Let me see you," Bella said.

Chains rattled as he stepped into the light. The first thing she saw was his bare foot. She watched as the color of his skin changed before her eyes. The color bloomed from an ashy gray to a pale peach. He moved closer to the light and was amazed at the transformation she was witnessing firsthand. His eyes were dark brown. No longer the blood thirsty red they had been for the past three years. She sobbed with relief at the sight of them. Bella had honestly believed she would never look into those eyes again.

"Oh God. It worked," she whispered.

"Bella . . . what's happening?" Teddy frowned and gazed at his hands as though seeing them for the first time in his life.

"I think . . . I think I found the cure," she said.

Teddy smiled for the first time in years. Some of his teeth had fallen out, but it didn't matter. He was alive. Truly alive.

"I have to take a blood sample just to make sure, but from where I'm standing, you look great."

Teddy gave her a shaky nod.

She looked at the room they were in. This wasn't a place for him now that he was coming back to life. It would serve as a reminder of the monster he had become and all of the awful things they'd said and done to each other in this dark place.

"Okay . . . okay. We need to change your accommodations. This room is unacceptable for you now," Bella whispered.

She needed to place Teddy in a different room. One with a shower so he could clean up and change into clean clothes. She took a huge risk by doing so, but she pulled the key out of her pocket. Her hand trembled as she placed it inside the lock. She carefully undid the chains that had bound him to this dismal room for three long years. The chains fell on the floor with a loud clank between their feet.

This was no longer a beast. She had brought this man back to life.

She placed a gentle hand on his wrist, amazed to find that his skin was warm to the touch. Teddy closed his eyes and basked in the sensation.

"Is this real? Is this really happening?" he whispered. He licked his lips and cleared his throat. It would take him time to adjust to speaking in coherent sentences again.

Bella nodded. "I think so. I'm not so sure myself. Sometimes I wonder if I'm sleepwalking half the time."

She lifted her gaze and their eyes met. She smiled, unable to pull herself away from him. But there were things they needed to do before she could make an announcement to everyone in the compound. She needed to run several blood tests to make sure everything was all right and that it was safe to bring him back upstairs.

"Come on. It's time to finally get out of this room," she said as she extended her hand out to him.

"With pleasure," he replied taking her hand and interlocking their fingers together.

"Follow me," Bella said.

Teddy nodded without a word.

He followed her into another room in the basement that was much cleaner than the one he had been in. This room had clean walls that had been painted a soft, eggshell white. There was a bed, a small desk, chair, and a bathroom.

She opened the bathroom door and turned on the shower. She grabbed a much-needed toothbrush and toothpaste and helped Teddy brush his teeth. She knew she was being reckless and insane. There were procedures and protocols she had to follow. But she threw caution to the wind. If this was how she died . . . then so be it. All she had wanted for the past three years was one more moment with Teddy and she was going to take it.

Once Teddy finished brushing, he looked at Bella, as though waiting for further instructions. He looked like a man that would've followed her to the gates of hell with a smile on his face.

Bella slowly removed her clothing and stepped into the steady stream of hot water that burst from the shower head. Teddy followed her lead. He quickly ripped his tattered clothes off and tossed them aside. He stepped into the shower with Bella and looked at her with wanting eyes.

Bella smiled at him and let the water wash over them. She watched as years of dirt, grime and blood ran down his body. She grabbed a bar of soap and carefully bathed him. All the while, Teddy's eyes remained fixated on Bella. When she was finished, she grabbed a small bottle of shampoo and washed his hair. More dirt and blood washed away and made its way down the drain. She rested her head against his chest and listened to his heartbeat. She listened to a strong and steady rhythm.

"Bella . . ." Teddy whispered. He leaned over and kissed the top of her head.

"I know. Just . . . I need a moment," she replied.

She looked up at him tracing his lips with her fingers. Lips she had kissed hundreds of times before. Unable to wait another moment she stood on the tips of her toes and kissed him. Softly at first. She let out a sob as she pulled away for a moment. Teddy wrapped his arm around her waist, lifted her and pressed her back against the wall. She tried to wrap her legs around him but the water had made things a little complicated.

But it didn't matter. He was alive. And they were together. That was all she had ever wanted.

BELLA WOKE UP IN THE MIDDLE OF THE NIGHT WITH A START. SHE squinted as she tried to make sense of where she was. Had she dreamed everything that had happened last night? She felt a warm body lying next to her. She placed her hand over his chest, feeling the strong heartbeat and the rise and fall of his steady breathing.

Teddy. Back from the dead.

She ran her fingers over his profile, amazed that he didn't stir at her touch. She still had so many questions. Tests to run.

Things she wanted to say to him now that he was alive. She glanced at their discarded clothes and felt her cheeks grow warm, remembering their tryst in the bathroom.

She let out a soft sigh and gathered her things, then got dressed in the dark, careful not to wake Teddy from his slumber. Bella hated leaving him like this, but there was still much work that needed to be done before she could tell everyone about what had happened and what she'd discovered. She found a syringe in her lab coat pocket and drew out a small sample of his blood.

"I'm sorry," she whispered as she pulled out the needle.

Teddy didn't move a muscle. He let out a soft snore and whimper as he rolled over to his side and continued to sleep.

She walked out of his room holding her breath, for fear of waking him, and then finally took several gulps of air after the door shut. Shaking her head, she punched in her code and flinched when she heard the soft beep and click of the door being locked. No matter how she felt about Teddy, everyone else's safety came first.

She went to her laboratory and ran a quick blood test on Teddy's sample. She placed a small droplet of blood in the microscope. She said a silent prayer before placing her eyes over the ocular lens.

The results were . . . normal.

Bella pulled herself away from her desk and let out a sob of relief. Three years of loving this man had paid off. Three years of exhaustive work and one mouthy gardener were to thank for the cure she'd stumbled across.

Bella made an announcement the following morning over the speaker system and asked everyone to join her in the living room. She couldn't remember the last time they were all in the same room together like this. The only one not able to attend in person was Zee. But Bella knew she would make her presence known.

Bella looked around the room and saw everyone's hopeful eyes on her. Neve, Gus, Red, Ajax, Sam, Will, Jack, and Briar—her friends. She would do just about anything to keep them safe and protect them. She couldn't fight as well as Neve or Gus, but she could do this for them. She gave them a sad smile and waited until they got settled.

Their group had gotten a lot smaller over the past several years. She remembered when there were dozens of them roaming these halls. They gave her the space and freedom to work, which was why she worked as hard as she did. She knew they had high hopes for her and the work she was doing. And for the first time she could give them exactly that. Hope. Tears swam in her eyes as she tried to put together everything she needed and wanted to say to them.

Once everyone was seated, she could get started.

"You're probably wondering why I've asked you all to be here. As you all know, I've been working hard with Teddy to find a cure for this virus," Bella said.

"You mean working hard *on* Teddy," Red said.

Bella rolled her eyes and said, "You know what I mean."

"Okay," Red said.

"Anyway, thanks to Briar's blood sample I can say with absolute certainty I've developed a cure for the Aetervia virus."

"A cure?" Neve echoed.

"Yes," Bella said.

Red leaned forward, all jokes and playfulness gone in an instant. "Do you have proof? Has it been put to the test?"

"Of course I have proof. You think I'd bring you all here for nothing? Zee, can you please patch a feed from the room next to Teddy's to the monitor here in the living room?" Bella said.

Zee remotely turned on the monitor in the living room and everyone saw Teddy. He was wearing a pair of white scrubs and slippers. He was carefully walking over to the mirror, studying his reflection. He gingerly touched his blonde hair and then his cheeks. But his skin was now tan, the way it used to be before the virus plagued his body.

"Holy fucking shit," Briar said.

"It's progressing slowly, but I'm hopeful he'll be completely cured in the next forty-eight hours."

"What does this mean?" Sam murmured.

"Yeah," Neve said. "How can we produce large quantities of this to give to other compounds around the world?"

"I don't know. I'm still running tests. I'm still in the preliminary stages. I want to develop a vaccine as well, something to protect the people who haven't been bitten. Viruses have a strange way of mutating, so I want to prepare for that should it happen. Briar would have to volunteer her blood regularly to create the batches we need. There is still a lot we don't know. But whatever I did worked. This is my first breakthrough in years."

"Amazing," Gus said.

"This whole fucking nightmare can be over soon," Sam said.

"Okay. Before we get all excited," Bella said, "let's wait until Teddy has been cured for at least a few weeks before we make any more announcements. But things look promising."

"I need a list of materials and any equipment you need to mass produce this as soon as you've verified your findings," Neve said.

Bella nodded. "I will. For now, all I need is time and space to do my work."

"And more blood samples from me obviously," Briar said.

"I'd rather wait until you're completely healed from your trauma. You just woke up from a coma. Eat, drink, get plenty of exercise, and rest. Once you've done that, then I will be comfortable drawing more of your blood."

"There you go. Doctor's orders. Go eat," Neve said.

"Aye, aye, Captain," Briar said with a salute. She turned to Jack and said, "I need a stack of pancakes. *Tout de suite, por favor.*"

"You got it," he replied.

Neve gave Bella a warm embrace. Bella wrapped her arms around her best friend and held her tight. This had been a long and arduous road for them all. But she had finally done it. She had kept her promise.

EIGHTEEN

NEVE DID A LITTLE EXPLORING AND AFTER A FEW FALSE STARTS, SHE eventually found Michael's old room. She never realized that he had only been a few rooms away from her parents' bedroom. No one had been inside his room since he disappeared with Lila that terrible night.

She sat on the corner of his bed and looked around. She was surprised to see how plain it was. No posters. No pictures. Or color. Almost as if he were just passing by with no plans to stay. Michael had been Charles' best friend. His right-hand man. But Neve knew the truth now. He'd never truly been her father's best friend; it had all been part of the web of lies. Still, why wouldn't he have decorated his room? Everyone else had. Neve frowned and studied the room some more. Something didn't feel right. She got up and pulled the bed sheets off the mattress. Nothing. She threw the mattress off the bed frame.

Nothing.

She knocked the night table over. Nothing. The less she found the angrier she became.

"You motherfucker," Neve hissed.

Michael had come into her home and destroyed everything she loved over a woman who didn't love him in return. A woman who only loved herself.

Neve ran her fingers through her hair and gasped for air. Her chest felt tight as though she had a boa wrapped around her. The room spun until she felt as though she would throw up. She forced herself to take a deep lungful of air, realizing too late that she was in the middle of a panic attack with no one here to help her through it. She took another breath and did that for a few minutes until she felt calm enough to continue searching Michael's room.

Except there wasn't anything in his room, and for some reason, that devastated her. She fell to the floor on her knees and landed with a hard thud. One of the floorboards popped up.

That's something.

Neve moved toward the loose board. Her hands trembled as she touched the piece of lacquered wood. A part of her didn't want to find anything hidden underneath. She was terrified of what she might find there. Another part wanted something . . . anything to justify what had happened to her family.

She pulled two of the boards away and found rolled up papers underneath the floorboards. Neve pulled them out and unrolled them.

"Blueprints?" she whispered.

She took a closer look and realized that they were the blueprints to The Orchard. It was rare that they had used paper. Almost everything was on a tablet or computer.

Why on Earth would he hide these?

She noticed something right away as she scanned over the blueprint. There was a new corridor on the first floor that wasn't supposed to be there.

Or was she missing something? Was this an early copy of The Orchard blueprints?

"Zee?" she said out loud, knowing her girlfriend was watching her every move.

Her voice came through clear as a bell over her communicator. "Yeah?"

"Are you seeing this?"

"Yes."

"Do me a favor. Can you do a side-by-side comparison of the original blueprint versus this one? Specifically, the first floor. I wanna know about this corridor."

"No problem. Let me pull it up real quick."

"All right."

"Corridor, first floor. Right?"

"Yeah. Here, maybe this will help." Neve held up the blueprint she had found and did her best to keep it straight for Zee to see.

"I'm not seeing it on the original blueprint," Zee replied.

"Fuck." Neve spat.

"What is in there?"

"Another way out of the compound. It's probably how Lila snuck out of here that night without anyone noticing," Neve said.

"Oh no."

"Yeah."

Neve grabbed the blueprints and went downstairs. She needed to see this with her own eyes.

She checked the blueprint. The corridor was supposed to be somewhere between the painting of a sunset that her mother had completed just before Neve was born, and a family portrait. She used to hate that picture; some of her teeth were missing, and she had pigtails. But the more she looked at it, the more she loved it. Her mother looked at Neve adoringly as though her daughter had hung the stars in the sky. Violet's dark brown eyes always crinkled when she smiled. At least that's what her father used to tell her. Charles was in the picture as well, looking at the camera with a soft smile.

They were a beautiful family or at least they were until her mother became infected with the Aetervia virus and turned.

"Anything there?" Zee asked, her voice bringing her back to the present.

"No. Just a solid brick wall," Neve replied.

She checked the blueprint again and there wasn't anything else. No instructions. No buttons or code to push into a keypad. A dead end.

"Maybe your father noticed and closed up the hallway?" Zee suggested.

Neve shook her head. She would've remembered something like that. She followed her father all over the compound like a little shadow. She would've remembered a corridor being closed up. This had to be it. She felt it in her gut. She stared at the wall for a while, hoping that she would notice something out of place. But it all seemed deceptively normal.

"I know that look," Zee said.

"Oh yeah?" Neve cocked an eyebrow.

"You're going to break that wall down," Zee said.

"Yep."

"Want Gus to bring you a sledgehammer?"

"Yep."

"Sounds like a solid plan. I'm on it," Zee said.

Neve smirked and tossed the blueprints on the floor. She took the sunset painting off the wall and carefully set it on the floor. Her heart dropped to her stomach when she saw that the wall was completely bare.

"Nothing," she whispered.

She walked over to her family portrait and giggled over her huge, goofy grin. She must've been three or four years old. She couldn't remember the last time she had a smile that big on her face or had been happy enough to want to grin like that. She set the ebony-framed picture on the floor next to her mother's painting and looked at the wall. There was a loose brick.

That's odd.

She ran her hand over the wall, feeling the rough texture against her skin for a moment. She pushed the loose brick back into place and gasped when she heard a soft whoosh and rumble as part of the wall slid to the side.

And there it was . . . a corridor, just like to one in Michael's blueprint.

"You son of a bitch," she whispered.

"Holy shit," Gus said as he walked up to Neve with the sledgehammer in tow.

"Give me that," she said as she stuck out her right hand.

Without missing a beat, Gus handed her the sledgehammer with one swift and graceful movement and took a step back; he knew better than to get in the middle of whatever Neve was about to do. She liked the weight of the sledgehammer in her hands. It made her feel anchored to this world.

She tightened her grip on the wooden handle and went down the dark corridor, uncertain of what she would find inside. A sudden chill ran down her spine as she stepped into the darkness. There were pipes and wires all over the walls, making her think of the forest in her nightmares. The ones she used to have over and over again when she was a child. It had been a long time since she'd had those types of dreams.

She kept walking with that sledgehammer in her hands, waiting for something to burst out of the walls and attack her. Her heart pounded against her chest, and she slowly made her way to the end of the corridor.

She set the sledgehammer down and ran her hands all along the wall until she found a switch. Her heart jumped when part of the wall slid back. When she stepped outside, she found herself in the back of the compound. The gentle breeze caressed her skin, and she looked toward the horizon, wondering if Lila had given her father a second thought as she snuck out of the compound.

"Dammit," she whispered.

"Neve? Are you all right?" Gus called out from the other side of the corridor.

"Yeah," she said.

"Do you need us to do anything? Want us to start blocking off this entrance?" he asked.

Neve nodded even though he couldn't see her. "We can start with that ASAP," she replied.

She stepped back inside, pushed the button, and closed the door. She picked up the sledgehammer and dragged it behind her as she made her way back inside. It felt as heavy as her heart did at that moment.

"I was worried for a second. I thought you were going to smash all of those pipes and wires," Gus said.

"Me, too, but I'm tired of kicking and punching everything. I just . . ." She took a shaky breath as she tried to finish her sentence.

"I know," Gus said, putting a gentle yet firm hand on her shoulder.

"Let's just have this blocked off. Who knows who'll come through that door."

"I'm on it," he replied.

"Thank you," she said.

"No problem."

Neve walked away from the hidden corridor, if only for a moment. She found a quiet corner in the living room and sat on the leather chair and stared off into space, trying not to think about the night she lost her father.

She would've done anything to save him or have one more minute with him. She closed her eyes and took a deep breath. She needed to talk to Jack and see if there was anything else he might've noticed Michael or Lila doing before he ran away.

She opened her eyes and stood.

She'd had her moment. It was time for action.

It was still early, so there was a chance that Jack would be outside working on the garden as promised. She felt a twinge of regret over punching him on the jaw, but at least he had stood there and owned up to what he'd done. In a strange way, that made her respect him a bit more.

She opened the garden door and was pleased to find Jack where she thought he'd be. He was kneeling in front of some newly planted strawberries and whispering as though he were having a conversation with them.

"Hey," she said, making her presence known.

He looked over his shoulder and gave her a short wave.

"Do you have a moment? I have a couple of questions," she said.

"Sure. What's on your mind?" Jack got up and dusted his hands off on his black jeans.

"I was hoping you could tell me the location of your old compound," she said.

"In Northern Texas. Middle of nowhere. You really need to know where it is to get there," Jack explained.

"Draw me a map," she said.

He frowned. "Why?"

"Isn't it obvious?"

He shook his head. "Neve, I'm telling you, begging you, please don't go. Stay away from her. All she will do is bring you sorrow."

"I'm tired of sitting around and waiting. Wondering if she'll come here. Bringing more of her poison to spread it into the world. This has to stop. Someone has to put an end to this."

Jack nodded. "I know my arrival messed everything up. I get it and despite everything that has happened between us, I respect you and how hard you work to keep everyone safe. But please don't go looking for her. Whatever you think you know about her? Her time here? She spent all that time suppressing her natural urges."

"Geez. What the fuck was she into?"

"That's what I'm trying to tell you. She's a monster," Jack said.

"I caught her talking to herself in the mirror once," Neve said. "She was touching and caressing her face, looking for wrinkles and muttering to herself. It was without a doubt the creepiest fucking thing I had ever seen in my life."

"She's incredibly vain. That was one of the reasons she experimented with different chemicals, trying to find a way to stay young forever. She didn't need any of that junk. You saw that picture of us together. She was beautiful."

"I know."

"Neve, she doesn't care," Jack said. "She created this virus, let it run rampant as she continued to run tests on people . . . sometimes without their consent. She ruined the lives of so many people and she will continue to do so until she finds her way to what she thinks is perfection, all without a second thought as to the destruction she's caused."

Neve growled in frustration and shouted, "Dammit, Jack. I know!" She let out a deep sigh. "I'm sorry. I just . . . I need to do something."

Jack ran his fingers through his hair. "Listen, if you wanna go, I'll take you there. But at least take a couple of days to think it through. You face her and then what?"

Neve glared at Jack but remained silent.

"It won't bring your parents back. It won't change anything," he said.

"I can stop her from hurting anyone else. We have to try," she said.

"You're not going to try anything. Lila is as good as dead."

"Maybe I just wanna talk to her," Neve said.

He snorted. "You almost punched a hole through a brick wall just so you could get your hands on my mother's notebook. Trust me; if you see her, she's a dead woman."

"I'll sleep on it for tonight only. Tomorrow, you'll have my answer," Neve said.

"Okay," Jack replied.

Neve went to her bedroom, thinking some time alone would help her put things into perspective. But all she had there were the same pale blue walls she had been staring at her whole life. The glow in the dark stars were still glued to the ceiling. She had never gotten rid of them.

Her room was rather plain . . . unlike Zee's. Her girlfriend's walls were painted in a deep burgundy. Rich and velvety with pictures taped to the walls. Places that Zee wanted to visit one day if they still remained. Neve loved being in Zee's room. It was like being inside her girlfriend's heart.

A lump formed in her throat, and the harder she tried to push it down, the more it made its presence known. Neve covered her face with her hands as a sob escaped her lips.

Jack was right. Face Lila and then what? As much as she wanted to kill her, she wasn't a murderer. She couldn't kill someone in cold blood. A zombie was different. That was all in self-defense against a monster.

This was different . . . or was it?

Neve didn't know. She wished her father was here. He'd know what to do.

She walked up to her window and opened it, letting the fresh air caress her skin. She looked at Zee's tower, knowing she was there working, barely getting any sleep. She didn't have to be alone tonight. She had a beautiful girl in a tower who loved her. She would be a fool to keep her waiting.

She pretended for a moment that Zee was a princess unable to escape. Neve the brave knight willing to risk it all for love. Wasn't that what she was doing now? Taking a risk?

Neve went into the tower and spent several hours in the arms of her love.

Neve and Zee lay together in bed, tangled in each other's arms. Zee wasn't sure where she began and where Neve ended. She noticed that Neve's brown eyes were staring off into the distance. Looking at something only she could see.

"Are you okay?" Zee murmured.

Neve shook her head. "No."

Zee untangled herself from Neve's limbs, pulled her legs up to her chest, and rested her chin on her knees. She listened as Neve talked to her about her current dilemma.

"Do you really want to go out there? You have no idea what it's like out in the world," Zee said.

"But don't you think it's time to go and see? I can take the truck," Neve said.

"What if you run out of fuel and can't come back?"

"I'll come back. I will always come back to you," Neve promised. Then pressed her lips against Zee's bare shoulder.

"You don't know that."

"What's the point of staying here and not doing anything?"

"We survive."

Neve got up and paced around the room. "And then what? Die? Dammit, Zee. I want . . ."

"What?" Zee's eyes scanned her girlfriend's face.

"Never mind," Neve said.

"No. Say it. What do you want?"

Neve pushed down the lump that had formed in her throat, as though bracing herself for what she was about to say.

"I want to live, Zee," she blurted out. "I want us to live together. I want to hold your hand while we walk outside. I want to go with you to one of those places taped on your wall."

"Those places are probably gone. Those are old pictures I found in some books or that I printed. And you know I can't leave," Zee whispered.

"Then why do you have them taped to your walls? You want to go somewhere someday, don't you?"

"I like having the pictures on the walls. But that doesn't mean I want to die for them. I don't need to see an old building that badly," Zee argued.

"We can go one day. But you have to at least try to take a step outside. At least walk around the garden with me," Neve said, her eyes filling with hope. A hope too big for Zee to carry.

"I can't leave," Zee whispered.

Neve shook her head, the disappointment evident in her eyes. "You *won't* leave. There's a difference."

"Fine. Whatever you wanna call it. I won't go," Zee said.

"Won't isn't the same as can't though. You can go."

"No, I can't!" Zee shouted.

Neve gasped. Zee had never raised her voice to her.

"Don't do this," she whispered. Zee licked her lips and wiped away the tears that stung her eyes. "Just stay here with me. We can live here together if you want."

"You don't understand," Neve said as she gathered her clothes and put them back on.

"Where are you going?" Zee asked.

"Back to my room. I don't want to say something I'll regret."

"Are you coming back?" Zee asked.

Neve sighed and rested her forehead against the cold steel door. She turned then and gave Zee a sad smile. "Of course I will. I love you. More than anything in this world."

Zee walked up to Neve and waited for her to say more. Neve caressed Zee's cheek. Zee held Neve's hand and pressed it harder against her skin.

"But?"

"I need time to think. I promise I will be back," Neve said.

"I love you," Zee whispered.

"Love you, too. I'll see you later." Neve kissed Zee on the forehead and left the sanctuary of the apartment.

Zee closed her eyes and let her go without a fight. Her arms felt numb as the warmth of Neve's touch vanished. She walked over to the window and looked up at the silver moon.

Could I? she wondered as she looked down at the ground. She watched as Neve walked out of her tower and ran her hands over her jet-black hair. Locks she had touched not too long ago. Now all she wanted was to bury her face in them and breathe in their scent.

The truth was that Zee wasn't mad. Neve had some valid points. But her fear was bigger than all of the facts in the world.

Was Zee willing to fight her fear all in the name of love? Or would she let it win and ruin her life?

Only time would tell . . .

The following day Zee went through her regular routine. She ran a diagnostic on Neve's droids and found nothing wrong with them. She uploaded an update on their software to make it more efficient. That took her most of the morning. She made herself a bowl of lime shrimp ramen noodles for lunch. Neve had brought her a box the last time she visited her. She ate as she checked the monitors, her expression growing serious when she turned her attention to the monitor showing the front gate. She slurped her noodles and put her glasses on.

"What the fuck?" she muttered.

She set down her bowl on the desk and zoomed in on the screen. She kept going until she got a clear view.

Zombies. Hundreds of them were ambling their way toward The Orchard. Men, women, children.

"No! Oh God. NO. Not here," Zee cried.

Zee's hand trembled as she turned on her communicator and called Neve. She was with Gus working on blocking off access to that secret corridor she had found on the first floor.

Even after their conversation the night before, she had to set her feelings aside and get to work.

"Neve, you need to see this," Zee said with a shaky voice.

"What's wrong?"

"Look at the monitor to your left."

Neve did as Zee asked, and a second later Zee patched a signal to that monitor next to where the sunset painting hung.

"What the fuck?" Neve whispered.

"I'm zooming in, so you can see who's all the way in the back," Zee said.

Neve peered at the screen and screamed in horror when she saw Lila's face. Lila rode in a hover car with the top down headed straight toward The Orchard.

"Is that her?" Zee asked.

"Yeah," Neve replied.

"What do we do?"

"Neve," Gus said, "she could still come through this entrance. We're not finished blocking off this corridor."

"I know. Just do what you can. If you find the wire that opens the outside door cut it, even if it means we're without power. Do whatever it takes to keep that door closed," Neve said.

"On it," Gus replied and then ran off into the corridor.

Zee prayed silently that he could find a way to keep that entrance closed.

"Where is everyone right now?" Neve demanded.

"Bella's in the lab with Teddy, running more tests on him. Briar's in her room. Jack's in the kitchen. Red and Ajax are in the living room. Will is in the bathroom taking a leak. Sam is reading a book in the garden. Does Teddy count as a person? Is he still technically dead?"

"I don't know, Zee. I'll figure that out later. For now, put everything on lock down. No one gets out. No one gets in. Ready all weapons. Warn everyone. Get the speakers ready. I have a few things I want to say to that bitch."

"Okay."

"Are any of your friends online at the moment? Anyone willing and able that can fly or drive here? Maybe we'll get lucky and someone actually has an old plane in their backyard. Anyone that can help us fight a psycho bitch from Hell with her own personal army of zombies."

"I'll find out. Just give me a second."

While Neve ran down the hallway, Zee's fingers clicked and tapped away against the keyboards. She checked online to see if anyone was logged on. Web access was a luxury. Not everyone could be online 24/7 like Zee. She would do everything she could to connect with someone—even if it killed her.

⊙ ⊙ ⊙

ONCE THE SPEAKERS WERE READY, NEVE TURNED ON HER COMMUNIcator. "Lila Beauchamp! Move another inch, and I swear that it'll be the last fucking thing you do."

Neve's heart hammered against her chest so hard and fast she thought it would burst through her ribcage. This wasn't how she imagined this happening at all. She thought she would be the one storming Lila's compound and avenging her parents. Even that was denied to her.

Lila stopped her car and raised her hand in the air. The hoard of zombies stopped moving almost immediately. Neve watched in horror as they gnashed their yellowed teeth at the air, as though angry that they had been commanded to stop.

How did she do that?

"If it isn't sweet, little Neve all grown up. Your voice is a lot deeper than I remembered," Lila said as she stepped out of her vehicle.

"What the fuck are you doing here?"

Lila clapped her hands excitedly, as though someone just surprised her with a birthday cake. "I wanted to show you my new batch of pets. They're much more obedient than the first set I made. These obey my every command. Isn't that wonderful?" Lila said in a saccharine voice.

"Why are you here?" Neve repeated.

Lila pretended to gasp in surprise. "I thought you knew." Then her face contorted in anger and she growled. "We have some unfinished business to take care of, you little bitch."

"Yeah, we do. Seeing as you're the one who infected my father with your virus and left him here to die."

Lila flinched and looked away as though the memory of that night caused her physical pain. "That night, that was an accident," Lila said.

Neve winced at the word. "An accident? Is that why you ran away without a word? Fuck you. You ruined my life."

"Enough talk! You know why I'm here. I want the apples."

"You will get those apples over my dead body." Neve growled.

"With pleasure," Lila said.

"Then what are you waiting for, bitch? Come and get 'em!" Neve said.

Lila got back in her hover car and gave the order to her zombies to march. She drove behind them slowly as if she had all the time in the world.

"Zee! You know what to do," Neve said.

"On it," she replied.

Zee readied the guns and ammunition and shot at all of the zombies when they reached the front gate.

Neve turned on her communicator and called Red. "Yeah."

"Ready all weapons. Get Velma prepped and any insane weapons you've been dying to play with. Go nuts," Neve said.

"Yes!" Red shrieked.

"Gus, get Will and Sam and secure the perimeter. Make sure there's no way for anyone or anything to sneak inside. Keep a close eye on that corridor on the first floor. She will try to use it. It's our only weak spot right now."

"On it," Gus said.

Neve patched her communicator over to Bella's and said, "Grab Teddy and Briar, then head up to Zee's tower. We need you to be in a safe place."

"But I can help. We can fight," Bella argued.

"This isn't a request. It's a direct order. I expect you to follow it," Neve said.

"Fine," Bella said.

"Neve, what are you going to do?" Zee asked.

"Fight. Protect you guys until the bitter end. That's what I'm good at," Neve replied.

"Be careful," Zee said.

"I will," Neve said.

With that having been said, she went to join Red on the parapet to defend The Orchard. Red brought every gun and rifle she could carry. Even Ajax was wrapped with a bunch of ammo. The poor dog whined and then lay down so Red could unwrap the ammo from his body.

"It's okay, buddy. You did good," she said sweetly as she gave him a quick peck on the nose.

Neve rushed to Red's side and looked over the wall. She couldn't believe her eyes. Hundreds of zombies heading toward The Orchard. Yet, a cool breeze caressed her shoulders, reminding her that the first day of summer would arrive soon. The grass was lush and green beneath their decayed feet. And somewhere in the chaos, her stepmother was trying to force her way back inside her home.

"Welcome to the party," Red said.

"Not the kind of party I would've planned for us," Neve replied.

Red chuckled. "Here. Saved you this." She handed an M-16 to Neve. "It's got a bit of kickback, and there's a ton of ammo, so go nuts."

Neve nodded.

"Single shots. Make 'em count."

"Will do."

"Do you want to go get the M Three Twenty?"

"No time. We'll stay here and do what we can," Neve said as she aimed and fired her weapon.

She felt a surge of pride as the zombie in jeans and ratty gray T-shirt fell to the ground with a soft thud. She wasn't that great at long range, but she blew off a few heads in a couple of minutes.

At least they had the land mines on the moat that she knew would go off without a hitch.

"Die! Die, you fuckers! DIE!" Red shouted. She let out a wild cackle as she continued to fire her weapon with aplomb. She pulled the trigger on Velma and whenever she had to reload, Neve took over. Zee let her know that Jack, Sam, and Will were on the other side of the compound shooting as many zombies as they could from that angle.

Neve focused all of energy and attention on the onslaught of zombies. So much so that she lost sight of Lila.

"Shit! Where is she?" Neve gazed quickly over the crowd of dead.

"I don't know," Red said.

"Zee! Do you see her?" Neve yelled.

"I tried to shoot at her remotely, but she made it past me. I think she went to the other side of the compound," Zee said.

"Didn't Jack and the others spot her?" Neve asked.

"She had a bunch of zombies protecting her. They surrounded her, and the guys couldn't get a visual of her. She snuck right past them," Zee said.

"Why is she going around the compound? That's not the way in," Red said.

Neve realized that Red had no idea about the corridor on the first floor.

"Fuck," Neve spat. Her heart dropped to her stomach. She ran to the other side of the compound as fast as her legs could carry her and watched in horror as the first few zombies trickled in through the corridor.

This was all happening too quickly. They had prepared for a few dozen zombies, not an army of them led by her psycho stepmother. There were hundreds there.

Neve used the M-16 and fired at' every zombie within her line of sight. More and more zombies pushed their way through the secret entrance.

"Oh God," she whispered. She turned on her communicator and hoped that everyone could hear her message. "Run! Everyone run! Head to Zee's tower if you can't find a safe exit. The zombies are inside the compound. I repeat, the zombies are inside the compound!"

"What?" Gus shouted.

A wave of relief washed over her when she heard Gus' deep voice.

"Fucking run! The zombies found a way inside!" Neve cried as she continued to shoot.

"Shit!" Gus spat.

"Okay, Neve. We'll meet you at Zee's," Red said.

Neve shot a few more zombies and then made a run for it.

Neve, Red, Gus, Will, and Jack met outside the tower.

"Wait. Where's Sam?" Red asked.

Jack shook his head and gave Will a look.

"We lost him on the way here. He stayed behind to make sure we made it here safely," Will replied.

"Dammit," Neve hissed.

She punched the code into the keypad. They all rushed inside. She closed the door and entered another code. One that couldn't be overridden should Lila try to use a program to hack her way in. Together they climbed up the stairs, made it through the seven steel doors until they reached Zee's door.

Neve knocked and Zee opened the door, then pulled Neve into her arms.

"Thank God you're all right," Zee said.

Neve patted her girlfriend gently on the back and whispered, "It's okay. I'm here."

Once they were all inside, Zee locked the door behind them. Neve buried her face into her hands. She gave herself a moment to mourn her friend, Sam. He was always so calm . . . and quick with a joke that would catch her off guard. He was always trying to get Neve to laugh and sometimes he failed miserably, but she appreciated the gesture. And now she would never see him again. Another life lost. She took a deep breath and tried to think of a way for them to get the rest of her friends out of here alive. She looked up and saw that all eyes were on her. The unasked question in their eyes as they stared at her:

What do we do now?

"I know. You don't have to say anything . . . I know," Neve said.

She turned and looked at the monitors, watching as a hoard of zombies clawed at the reinforced steel door outside the compound's gate.

"We have to figure out how to kill Lila, the zombies, and survive," Neve said.

"That's a tall order," Jack said. "How are we supposed to do that? We're surrounded."

"There has to be one place that's free and clear of everyone. A place we can sneak into," Neve said.

Zee sat on her desk and tapped on the keyboard a few times. "Lila's at the apple orchard door trying to get inside."

"Yeah. I figured that's where she'd be," Neve said.

"She doesn't have the code to get in, right?" Gus asked.

"She might have the one my dad used seven years ago," Neve replied, "but I've changed it a few times since then. So at least she won't be able to get in that easily. But I don't know what type of technology she's developed. She could have the tech to hack her way in."

"We need weapons. I left some of my best rifles on the parapet. I brought what I could carry," Red said as she scratched Ajax's chin.

"I have a few guns in here, but not enough ammo for everyone," Zee said.

"Okay, it's great to hear you all throw these ideas around," Briar said, "but truth of the matter is that we're all fucking trapped in here. There's only one way in and out of here." Briar pointed to the door.

Neve knew if they didn't do something soon, they would all die in this tower. It would probably take a few weeks, but one by one they would die of starvation. At least that's how she felt until she gazed out the window and then at Zee's long hair. Her blonde braids trailed behind her like strands of golden rope.

"Uh oh. I know that look," Bella said.

"Zee, do you have any rope?" Neve looked around.

"I think so." Zee looked under the sink and found a short piece of old rope.

"That won't work." Neve went to the window and looked down. There were a few zombies ambling aimlessly down below, but nothing they couldn't handle once they reached the bottom.

"Are you thinking what I think you're thinking?" Jack smiled.

"We can climb out the window," Neve said.

"How? There's no rope," Will said.

"There is something else that might work," Neve replied. Then everyone slowly turned their heads toward Zee.

Her eyes widened in surprise, and they darted nervously from side to side. "What? Do I have something on my nose?" Zee quickly wiped the nonexistent smudge off her nose.

"Zee, can I talk to you in private?" Neve whispered.

"Yeah, sure," she replied.

Neve and Zee stepped into the bedroom. Everyone peeked inside to eavesdrop on the conversation. Neve closed the door and locked it for good measure. She had no idea how to explain to Zee what she needed to do. So she figured the best thing to do was blurt it out and hope for the best.

"Zee, there's no easy way for me to say this, but I'm going to cut your hair."

"What?" Zee touched her hair.

Neve rushed to her and held her hands. "I know, sweetie. I know it's a lot to ask, but we'll die in here if I don't do it. I'll only cut from the shoulders down. I can tie your hair into knots and that should be enough for us all to climb out of your tower."

Zee let out a soft whimper, then covered her lips.

Neve quickly wrapped her girlfriend in a warm embrace.

"I'm so sorry. I promise, if we make it out of this alive, I will spend the rest of my life making it up to you. I swear," Neve whispered.

"It's not that. It's just. Oh God, this is going to sound so stupid now that I'm thinking about saying it out loud. It was one of the first compliments you gave me when we first met, so I've been kind of attached to my hair ever since."

Neve pulled herself away and giggled. "Is that why you think I love you? Because of your hair?"

Zee shrugged.

Neve smiled through the tears that stung her eyes. "Oh, Zee. You're smart, kind, beautiful, and honest. You could be bald, and I would still have nothing but love for you."

"Really?"

"Absolutely," Neve replied.

"You're not just saying that so I'll let you cut my hair?"

"While we really need it right now, I meant every word I said."

Zee closed her eyes and took a deep breath. "Okay. Cut it," she said.

"Are you sure?" Neve whispered.

"Yeah. Do it now before I change my mind," Zee said.

"I love you," Neve whispered.

"I love you, too," Zee replied.

Neve pulled out her dagger and grabbed a large chunk of Zee's hair. She took a deep breath as she slowly got to work. It took several minutes to cut Zee's hair from the shoulders down.

Zee whimpered, but then took a deep, shaky breath.

"You're okay," Neve said in a soft soothing voice.

Zee gingerly touched the ends of her hair and just as Neve promised, everything was okay. Neve leaned forward and kissed Zee on the lips, then on the tip of her nose and then on her forehead.

"Thank you," Neve said.

"You're welcome."

Neve stepped out of the room, and in an instant, she went from being a lover to a warrior.

"Gus, can you help me tie Zee's hair into knots? Make them good and strong. We're all going to climb down."

"All at once?" Will's eyes widened.

"One, maybe two at a time, depending on how it holds up," Neve replied.

Gus worked with Neve, and together, they tied Zee's hair into climbing rope.

"Neve, are you sure this is a good idea?" Zee looked worried.

"Right now, it's the only idea I've got that gives us all a chance to get out of here alive. Whether it's good or bad is still up for debate," Neve replied.

"What about me?" Zee asked.

"You stay here with Teddy. Same goes for you two." Neve pointed at Briar and Bella.

"Why the fuck do we have to stay here? I can still point a gun and shoot it just like anyone else," Briar argued.

"Because your blood holds the cure to this disease. Bella is the only one that knows how to turn it into a cure, and I like to think that Teddy would like to not be a zombie again," Neve said.

"All valid points, but Teddy and I aren't staying here. We're coming with you," Bella argued.

"Bella it's not safe," Neve said.

"It's not safe anywhere. But I'm not going to sit here and pretend to be a damsel in distress," Bella said.

"Dammit! I'm trying to keep you all alive," Neve shouted.

"And I'm telling you that we either all go together or I sneak out of this tower and follow you. Which do you prefer?" Bella crossed her arms over her chest.

Neve took a deep breath and threw her arms up in mock surrender.

"Fine. Zee, you can stay here if you want. Briar and Ajax can stay with you until we come back. You will be the eye in the sky. Spread the message to your friends online. Tell them it's an emergency. Tell them we have the cure for the virus. If they want it, they have to come here and get it."

"Got it," Zee nodded and sat at her desk.

Neve threw the window open and welcomed the fresh air that rushed into the room. She made the mistake of looking down. Her vision swam for a moment and she took several deep breaths to steady herself.

"I'll come back for you when this is over," Neve said. She hoped it was a promise she could keep.

NINETEEN

ZEE COULDN'T STOMACH THE IDEA OF LEAVING HER SANCTUARY. IF it made Neve feel better, then she would gladly tolerate Ajax's shedding and drooling. Did Neve really expect her to climb out a window . . . using her own hair as rope?

Hell. No.

She typed a message as fast as her fingers could manage.

Hello Friends:

We've never met in person, but throughout the years, we've maintained what I like to call a semblance of friendship.

Today, I'm sending this message asking for your help. We're running out of time, so I'll keep it brief. My friends and our compound are under attack hundreds of zombies. I've attached a map and our coordinates to this message. We also have the cure for the Aetervia virus. Please help.

Zelda Rampion aka Rampion2389

She cut and pasted the letter in every single email, forum, website and social media page that was still online and functional. It was the least she could do. Spread the word. She tapped her screen a few times and adjusted the cameras. She watched as Neve and her friends slowly made their way down the side of the tower. Zee shuddered and tried to shake the horror off her body.

Nope. Just . . . nope.

Zee couldn't believe that Neve had cut her hair. She self-consciously touched her head a few times and then forced herself to stop otherwise she wouldn't be able to concentrate on the task at hand. The constant throbbing in her head was gone and she felt lighter. As if she could fly if she really wanted.

A loud beep brought her attention back to the computer.

Someone replied to her message.

GreyDove211: Is it true?

Rampion2389: Which part?

GreyDove211: That you have a cure for the disease.

Rampion2389: Yes, it's true. We were able to cure one of our friends. He's been a zombie for three years, and he's been cured. I have video I can stream right now if you want visual proof.

GreyDove211: What's the situation?

Zee then explained everything that was happening.

GreyDove211: I've downloaded the map. We'll be there as fast as possible.

Rampion2389: Thank you so much.

Zee's heart leapt to her throat. For as long as she had been at the compound, it had been her job to keep their location a secret. She could give a coded signal and communicate with half the country, but no one had ever known where they were. That was about to change.

GreyDove211: You're not too far from us. I'll spread the word and get some of my friends to help. Just sit tight.

Easier said than done, she thought.

TWENTY

NEVE COULDN'T BELIEVE HOW STRONG ZEE'S HAIR WAS. EVERYONE was able to climb down without any trouble. Neve was the first one to climb down the tower. She pulled out her machete and killed a few zombies that were nearby. Gus climbed down moments afterwards and joined in on the fight to make sure no one was injured when they reached the bottom of the tower.

Once they were all on solid ground, they needed to form some type of plan.

"First thing we need are weapons and ammo," Neve said.

"Now you're talking," Red replied. She rubbed her hands together with a gleeful smile on her face.

"What does everyone have weapons-wise right now?" Neve looked at each of them.

Red was traveling light with only three guns and a shotgun on her as well as ammo. Gus had his rifle. Bella and Teddy shared a gun they had found in Zee's apartment. Teddy still looked a little unsteady on his feet, but to be fair he had just been brought back to life a couple of days ago. Neve had a machete and an M-16. Will had his rifle. Jack had a knife. But they would need much more than that.

"Typical. Bringing a knife to a gun fight." Red handed her extra guns to Jack and Teddy. "Do you even remember how to use this?" Red looked at Teddy.

Bella snatched the gun from his hands, cocked it, and had it ready for him. "Just aim and shoot at anything that's not us. I'll handle any of the zombies he misses."

Teddy nodded.

"All right, I'm going to take Fluffy Bunny with me," Red said as she cocked the shotgun.

"Fluffy Bunny?" Teddy echoed.

"Imagine having to tell your friends that you were defeated by a woman with something called the Fluffy Bunny. Now that is a fate worse than death. And I have plans on using it to my advantage. Or if I kill a bunch of zombies with my shotgun, people will tell tales of Red Rousseau and The Fluffy Bunny . . . Zombie Slayer."

Jack snorted and chuckled. "You're fucking crazy. You know that, right?"

"Tell me something I don't know." Red gave him a playful wink.

"Let's go," Neve said. Together, they went back into the compound.

Oh my God.

The smell of rotting flesh and blood overrode her senses. There were zombies everywhere. Ripping things off the walls, knocking things down. Destroying the furniture, pictures, their food . . . everything. Violating their home.

Red was the first one to spring into action. "Finally! I get to have some fun." She let out a whoop of delight and shot at every single zombie in sight.

Gus followed Red's lead, and together they paved the way for everyone else in the group. They hacked and blasted their way to the armory. There, Neve punched her code into the keypad. Her fingers trembled causing her to accidentally push the wrong number. The light turned bright red and denied them access. She tried again as everyone else behind her protected her from the oncoming zombies.

"Hurry the fuck up!" Red shouted as she fired her shotgun at a zombie that was gnashing its teeth as it ambled toward them.

"I'm going as fast as I can," Neve said as the light turned green, and the door slid open.

They pushed their way in and locked the door behind them. "Okay. Now we're in here and they're out there," Jack said.

"My father thought of everything when he built this place," Neve said.

"Not everything since he clearly didn't plan on having a psychotic wife who could control zombies," Red said.

"She's not wrong," Will said.

Neve ignored their chatter, grabbed a folded step stool and unfolded it. She pushed up a panel on the ceiling and set it aside. Reaching up, she pulled down an old, dusty rope ladder. Tiny bits of dust and dust-bunnies floated all around them for a few moments.

"We're getting out of here through the vents," she explained.

"And then what?" Red began grabbing as many weapons as she could carry.

Jack reached for a rifle that Red was eyeballing. She bared her teeth and growled.

"Okay, I guess that one's yours. I'll grab this nice . . . shotgun." Jack smiled and stepped away from the one Red wanted.

"Smart move," Gus whispered.

"Kill as many zombies as you can as you guys make your way to the garage. Get the truck, and get everyone out of here," Neve said.

"What are you going to do?" Bella snatched up a box of shotgun shells and gave them to Teddy to carry.

"I'm going after Lila. We've got some unfinished business to attend to," Neve said.

"But what about the cure? Zee's upstairs promising people that we have the cure for the disease," Bella said.

"And we do. That's not a lie. Plus, we're kinda fucking busy trying to not die. You know what I mean?" Neve replied.

Neve pressed the blue button on her shoulder and called her droids. Within a few minutes, they had zipped through the chaos and wreckage. She winced as she heard them banging and clanking against the metal air vents. She hoped they weren't damaged beyond repair. She would need their help to get through the compound now that it was overrun with zombies. They finally made their way to Neve in the armory. She picked up TRe-Z and carefully placed it inside an old black backpack she found on the floor.

Gus frowned, recognizing the droid Bashful. He knew what the droid was capable of. "What exactly are you going to do?"

"I'm going to destroy the orchard. She wants the apples, so I'm going to make sure she watches it go up in flames before I slit her throat." Neve turned her attention to Jack. "I hope you don't have any objections to me killing your mother."

Everyone in the room glared at Jack.

He raised his hands in mock surrender. "I won't kill her myself, but I won't get in your way."

"You better not," Gus said.

"Noted," Jack replied.

"Are we done talking and holding each other's fucking pussies?" Red demanded. "I, for one, would like to hurry the fuck up and kill some zombies. I'm not planning on dying today."

Neve grabbed a box of wires and C-4 and put them in the backpack with TRe-Z. She put the straps over her shoulders and braced herself for what was to come. "Let's go."

Together and armed, they climbed up the rope ladder and squeezed their way into the vents. Her droids followed closely behind them, awaiting her commands. Neve ignored the sense of panic and dread she felt as she crawled forward. It felt like the walls were closing in against her.

She took several deep breaths and focused on the task at hand: getting her friends out of The Orchard alive. She ignored all of the sweat that streamed down her body as well as the dust and dirt that clung to her skin with every inch she moved.

They all crawled until they reached an intersection. To the left was the garage. To the right the apple orchard and almost certainly, Lila.

Neve paused for a moment, causing Gus to bump his head against her left thigh. A droplet of sweat fell off her forehead and landed on her left hand with a soft splat.

"Sorry," he whispered.

"Why did you stop?" Red's voice floated forward.

"Making a choice," she whispered.

"And?" Gus asked.

Neve had two seconds to make a decision. Go with her friends and leave this place forever. Forget Lila and everything that happened in The Orchard. A fresh start.

Or . . . avenge her parents. She knew there was a chance that she would die trying but it was a risk she was willing to take.

"You guys go left. Keep going straight and then make the first right you see. That will lead you to the garage. Take the truck and get everyone out of here."

"What about you?" Gus asked.

"If you can find me alive, then yeah, come get me. But if you can't reach me, keep going."

"There's no way I'm doing that, Neve," Gus argued.

"You have to," Neve countered.

"Hey, what's going on up there?" Will called. "Why have we stopped?"

"I don't know," Teddy said.

"Don't worry about me," Neve said.

"Dammit, Neve. Be careful," Gus said.

"Give her hell," Jack said.

"Will do," Neve said and made a right turn.

With TRe-Z in her backpack and her droids following closely behind her, Neve carefully made her way to the apple orchard through the vent. After a while, covered in dust, sweat and God only knew what else, she finally reached her destination. She found a grated panel and pulled it out of its place. She sent her droids to scan the area for her. Once she was sure that there wasn't anything or anyone nearby, she crawled out of her hiding place and let herself fall on the floor with a soft thud. She ran toward the wall and pressed her back against it. Her heart hammered against her chest so hard she was almost certain it would burst out of her ribcage. She gasped for air, her lungs feeling constricted and tight. Taking a deep breath, she forced herself to move from her hiding place.

As soon as she reached the hallway, she found a male zombie in tattered clothes dragging its decaying corpse toward her. Its jaw had fallen off and was dangling by a thin tendon as it moved toward her. She aimed her M-16 at its head and put the monster out of its misery.

The closer she got to the apple orchard, the more zombies she encountered. Her weapon was almost out of ammunition by the time she found Lila standing in front of the orchard door.

"Stupid door. Open dammit," Lila muttered as she tried a different set of numbers on the keypad.

Neve stepped out of her hiding place and remained quiet as she watched her stepmother struggle with the door. Lila had a zombie on each side of her standing guard. They were just staring off into space not doing anything, which meant that Lila had a strong hold on this new batch of zombies. Even from behind, Lila looked different. Her hair was no longer brown and shiny. It was knotted and had gone gray, and from where Neve was standing, she could tell that Lila had lost at least twenty pounds. She looked gaunt and hollowed out.

"Looking for something?" Neve said.

Lila gasped and turned around.

Whoa.

Lila didn't look anything at all like Neve remembered. Lila's skin was riddled with fine wrinkles, and her blue eyes were dark and sunken in. Her lips were pale, dry, and cracked. It was hard to see all the changes from afar, especially through a small monitor. But now it was obvious that the past several years had not been kind to Lila.

Lila narrowed her eyes at Neve and bared her teeth at her like a rabid animal. "Shocking . . . isn't it?"

"What happened to you?" Neve whispered.

"This is what happens a week after my serum wears out. Do you see why I need to go inside The Orchard? I need those apples. I can't continue to look like this," she said as she motioned at her face.

"Do you really expect me to give you those apples? After everything you've done? You've literally destroyed the world. You certainly destroyed mine . . . "

"I need them!" Lila shouted. She pounded her fists against the steel door. "Charles would've given them to me," she whispered.

"You shut your whore mouth about my father," Neve said. "You're not leaving this place with those damned apples."

"You're willing to die for them? To let your friends die? Give me the apples, and you'll all walk away unharmed."

"You're a liar. I know you have no intention of letting us leave this place alive, so save it for someone who will believe your bullshit."

Lila opened her mouth to say something but Neve didn't want to hear it.

"Go," Lila whispered.

Neve frowned in confusion, wondering what Lila meant. But then she saw the two zombie guards spring into action. Neve aimed her rifle at them and fired her weapon twice, taking them down with relative ease. This was what she was trained to do, and Lila knew that all too well. But those two zombies were just a distraction.

Lila rushed at Neve and tackled her to the ground. The rifle fell, and Neve landed with a loud thud, knocking her head against the floor. Her vision swam for a moment but she quickly pulled herself out of it. Lila shrieked as she clawed at Neve's face with her long, sharp nails. Neve cried in pain with each scratch, the hot, sticky blood streaming down her cheek, instilling a sense of panic in her. She wrapped her hands around Lila's wrists and held her back, but was surprised at Lila's strength. In desperation, Neve head-butted Lila and crawled away from her.

Her stepmother tried to tackle her like before but Neve got up and side-stepped her like a bullfighter. She lost her balance for a second but quickly found her footing.

Lila growled in anger and tried again. Neve pulled back her fist and punched Lila on the cheek. Her stepmother groaned in pain, falling to the floor and massaging her wounded face, which turned beet red as she let out an angry howl.

Neve grabbed her rifle and aimed her weapon at Lila's knees.

She wasn't ready to kill her just yet. She wanted her to suffer like her parents had so many years ago.

Neve pulled the trigger twice without a moment's hesitation. Lila screamed in agony.

"Look at what you've done," Lila howled. Her hands trembled as she tried to touch her mangled knees, blood dripping from them and puddling on the floor.

"You deserve everything that has happened to you," Neve said.

"I hate you. I've always hated you," Lila hissed.

"Why?" Neve whispered.

"You wouldn't understand," Lila said.

"Try me."

Lila groaned; she looked like she was ready to pass out from the pain.

"You had your whole life ahead of you . . . and I had nothing. I was glad when I learned that my virus killed your mother. It gave me a chance with Charles. A chance to gain access to his precious orchard. Those apples would have been worth it all, but the bastard wouldn't let me near them, hoarding them for himself. I gave him everything but even that wasn't enough. Nothing I ever did . . . it was never enough."

"Don't you dare talk about my parents," Neve growled.

Neve then used the butt of the rifle and hit Lila on the face a few times until her stepmother passed out. Once Neve knew Lila was out cold, she punched in her code and opened the orchard doors.

When they opened, Neve was greeted with the scent of fresh air and the crisp bite of apples. She hated herself for what she was about to do. But she couldn't let anyone else get a hold of these apples to recreate Lila's formulas.

Neve grabbed Lila's arm and dragged her limp body into the orchard. She kept going until she reached the center of the apple orchard and pushed her stepmother's limp body against the tree. She held her upright while she searched for some duct tape in her backpack with the other hand. Neve tied Lila to an apple tree with duct tape. She put C-4 on some of the trees on the orchard and connected them all to Tre-Z with wires the droid had hidden inside.

Lila groaned as her eyes fluttered open. She looked down and gasped, realizing that she was bound. "Good. You're awake," Neve said.

"You don't understand," Lila whispered.

"I don't understand? Is that your excuse? I was fifteen years old. I had to watch my father become infected with the fucking disease *you* created. Watch him become a monster. I had to chop off his head. Don't fucking talk to me about *understanding*." Neve then she plucked a perfectly bright red apple from the tree.

Neve pried Lila's mouth open. Her stepmother struggled but Neve's grip was as hard as steel. She shoved an apple into Lila's mouth and gave her a gentle pat on the cheek.

"An apple for the road ahead," Neve said in a sweet tone.

Neve rose and walked out of the orchard. Once the doors closed behind her, she found herself alone. Truly alone for the first time since it all began. She'd lost so much through the years, they all had. And for what? For a crazed woman's obsession with her beauty? For an orchard full of coveted apple trees? In the end, it hadn't been enough for Lila. It never would have been and now Neve stood in the aftermath of her insanity, alone. She covered her face and let herself cry. For her parents, her friends, and for what she was about to do.

TWENTY-ONE

It was hard for Zee to watch everyone fighting. Some of them came close to either being bitten or losing a limb but so far so good. She kept using the weapons she controlled remotely from her tower and fired when she saw someone in trouble.

"Right there. Shoot," Briar said as she pointed at the monitor.

"Gotcha," Zee said and remotely fired her weapons, saving Will and Jack from a zombie bite.

"They're almost at the garage," Zee said.

"Thank God. We gotta get the fuck outta here," Briar said.

Zee's eyes remained mostly on Neve. She couldn't explain why, but she was particularly worried about her safety. Having Lila in the compound changed the energy around Neve. Even The Orchard felt different. It was as if Lila brought darkness with her wherever she went.

How could one person cause so much mayhem? Destroy so many lives? Bring chaos to the world and still remain fixated on one thing?

Zee would never understand.

"I hope I never do," she whispered.

Ajax growled at the door. Zee gasped and turned toward the sound. She looked at her monitor and tapped a few keys on the keyboard to change the view on the screen. Something was going on right outside her door.

Oh. My. God.

Several dozen zombies had broken down the first door and were pounding on the second door. There were still another six steel doors and a small elevator they would have to go through to get to Zee, Briar, and Ajax, but she couldn't help breaking into a cold sweat. Suddenly, the walls were closing in, and the room spun. A tiny bit of bile rose up her throat and she had to take several deep breaths to push it all down. This wasn't the time to have a panic attack.

"Zee, are you okay? What's wrong?" Briar touched her shoulder.

"The zombies have broken down the first steel door. They broke the keypad and it accidentally opened it. This new batch of zombies are smart. They might figure out how to open all seven doors," Zee said.

"Fuck," Briar spat. "Yeah."

"What's the plan?"

"We can either stay here and hope the doors hold until Gus gets here with the truck," Zee replied. "Or make a run for it and fight our way out of here until we catch up with Gus and the rest."

"I like the fighting part. But don't you have guns out there you can fire remotely?"

"Yeah, but I've used a lot of ammo, and we'll run out of that eventually. This was only supposed to be for a small batch of zombies, not a whole fucking army of them."

"Where are the others right now?"

Zee checked the monitor. They had reached the truck and were getting inside.

"Tell them to swing around here and pick us up. We're climbing down the tower," Briar said.

Zee nodded.

"Do you have a backpack or something for Ajax? You know Red will have a fucking fit if we leave him behind," Briar said.

"Yeah."

"Okay. Let's do this," Briar said.

Zee turned on the communicator and spoke to Gus. She asked him to stop by the side of the tower and pick them up.

"No worries. We're not leaving without you guys," Gus said.

She was ready to turn off her monitor when she saw Neve and Lila fighting. That woman was trying to claw Neve's eyes out. "No!" Zee cried.

"What?" Briar followed Zee's eyes.

"Neve's in trouble."

"Don't you have a gun or something in that room?" Briar yelled.

"No. I never thought anyone would want to attack the apple orchard. I focused all of my attention on the front gates and the perimeter surrounding the compound."

She watched helplessly as Neve fought for her life. "I have to go to her," Zee whispered.

"How?"

"I'm going. I'll climb out the window."

"Are you crazy? We're surrounded by zombies, and Gus isn't here yet," Briar said.

"You can stay and wait. Your blood has the cure. But I can still go and try to help," Zee said.

"You're fucking crazy," Briar said.

Zee grabbed her gun, a round of ammo, and her holster.

She hadn't worn it in years, but it still fit her like a glove when she wrapped it around her waist. She slipped her gun into the holster and the extra ammo in her pocket.

Zee looked out the window. A gust of wind rushed past her and whipped her short hair. She took a deep breath of that fresh air. Then she looked down. Her throat closed at the height.

"Neve needs me," she whispered. A wave of nausea rushed through her as she thought about what she was about to do. "Oh God. I think I'm gonna throw up."

"Good. Blow chunks all over the fucking zombies. At least make sure it's on their eyes. That should keep those motherfuckers from spotting you," Briar said.

"Not helping!" Zee said.

Her legs trembled as she sat on the ledge and carefully made her way down the wall. She repeated Neve's name over and over again in her head each time she grabbed hold of her hair and climbed down the side of the tower.

TWENTY-TWO

Neve closed her eyes and thought about her parents. All of the memories they had shared before the zombies. Mostly, the sound of her mother singing or laughing at something her father had said or done. Before death engulfed their lives.

"It's time," she whispered. She pressed the red button that activated Tre-Z. A loud, deafening boom shook the building to its core and reverberated through Neve's body. A few bricks slipped off the wall and knocked her unconscious.

For a moment, everything was quiet. She was finally at peace.

Neve opened her eyes and frowned. There was a clear sky above her with some perfect white clouds slowly crossing from one side to the other.

She sat up and shouted in surprise. Her head banged against something hard.

"Where am I?" she whispered as her hands touched what was immediately above her.

It was smooth and cold. She gasped in surprise when she realized that it was glass. She was inside a glass coffin. She looked down and realized that her clothes were different. Instead of her regular clothes and armor, she wore an ivory white Anjou gown. It featured rich brocades and lavish trims. The off-white sleeves ended in rounded shoulders.

She lifted her hands and tried to push the coffin lid open. But it wouldn't budge.

"No," she whimpered.

She pounded her fists against the lid until her hands bled. She pushed her hands against the glass, leaving behind bloody handprints. Nothing worked. "Help me!" she cried.

Just when she was ready to give up, she heard a soft rustle. She heard someone muttering about the noise. She didn't care what they were complaining about as long as they got her out of this coffin. Then she saw seven men peer into the coffin. They were dwarves. They reminded her of someone . . . or something, but she couldn't quite figure out where she knew them from.

"Help me. Please," she said as she pressed her bloodied hands against the glass. They all shook their heads and walked away.

"Don't leave me here!" she cried. Neve pounded her fists against the clear tomb, hoping that it would be enough to break it and set her free.

Neve groaned as her eyes fluttered open. Her head throbbed. She touched the back of her head, and when she checked her hand, it was sticky with her blood. She tried to get up, but was too weak to stand. Neve watched a zombie crawl toward her. Its legs were missing, and it had one eye dangling out of its skull.

For a split second, Neve wondered what it would be like to lie completely still and let it kill her. To stop fighting.

A gunshot fired, and the zombie's skull was eviscerated. Blue-black blood splattered against the walls, floor, and all over the lower half of Neve's body.

"Get the fuck away from my girlfriend," Zee said.

Neve's eyes widened in surprise.

Zee was out of her tower. Neve couldn't help but grin when she saw the frightened look on Zee's face. She looked as shocked as Neve to be out of the confines of her apartment.

Zee lowered her gun and put it back in its holster. She rushed to Neve's side and carefully caressed her cheek.

"Are you okay?" Zee smoothed Neve's hair from her damp forehead.

"No," Neve whimpered.

"Anything I can do to help?"

"No." Neve covered her face with her hands as tears fell freely down her cheeks.

"Are you sure?"

"No," Neve whispered.

"Shh. It's okay. I'm here." Zee gently wiped Neve's tears away. "Come on, let me help you up." She held Neve's hand and helped her stand.

Neve was still a little unsteady on her feet, but she stood with Zee's help.

"You left your tower," Neve said.

"Briar helped. I think she has a future as a motivational speaker," Zee said.

Neve smirked and then winced. Her head hurt like hell. "Your friends? The ones online?"

"Some of them saw my message, and they're on their way."

"Everyone's okay?"

"I think so. Briar and Ajax were still in the tower waiting for Gus and the others. I haven't heard anything that leads me to think otherwise."

Not wanting to take any chances, Neve turned on her communicator. "Gus, are you there?"

There was a momentary crackle of static and then Gus' loud voice came through clear as a bell. "Neve! I'm here. We all made it out. Do you want us to come back for you and Zee?"

"Yeah. We're all the way in the back of the compound near the orchard. Come get us," Neve said.

"On our way," Gus said.

Neve let out a sigh of relief knowing her friends were all right. She spared a moment and a prayer for poor Sam. She would miss her friend.

Hand in hand, Neve and Zee opened the apple orchard doors and were met with a giant wave of thick black smoke. Neve coughed and waved the smoke away to no avail.

SNe-Z zipped up next to them and blew the smoke away with one loud *sneeze*.

Neve arched an eyebrow at her droid. "Why didn't you tell me you could do that?"

SNe-Z twirled around like a puppy that had learned a new trick.

Neve stepped into the apple orchard and tried not to sob at the sight of the trees. It was all destroyed beyond repair.

"I'm so sorry, Neve," Zee whispered.

"It's okay. I had to do it," Neve replied.

"Where's Lila?"

"I don't know."

"You think she got away?" Zee whispered.

Thump, thump, thump.

Neve's heart dropped to her stomach when she heard the sound. Then she saw Lila's head roll over to them and stop between Zee's feet.

Lila's crone-like face stared at them in horror with half an apple still lodged between her teeth. "Remind you of anything?" Neve looked at Zee.

"Awww. The day we first met," Zee said sweetly, as though Neve was remembering a rainbow and not chopping her zombie mother's head off.

"Talk about our relationship coming full circle," Neve said in a dry tone. She kicked Lila's head into the burned orchard.

"I didn't know you were a romantic."

"I'm not."

"Lucky I love you anyway," Zee said.

"Me too."

"What happens now?" Zee's eyes were on the burned trees.

"We're going to kill the zombies still inside the compound," Neve replied, "salvage what we can, help Bella make more of that cure, and share it with the world."

"And then? What happens after that?" Zee looked at Neve.

Neve reached out to the woman she loved and held her hands in hers. Neve placed a gentle kiss on Zee's knuckles. Even in the middle of all this fire and decay she only had one thing on her mind.

"We live," Neve said.

"Yeah. That sounds like a good plan."

"I love you. I want to be wherever you are. Whether it's here or out there in the world. I just want to be with you," Neve said.

Zee gave her a warm smile. Her lips trembled softly as she whispered. "I'd like that too."

Neve kissed her on the lips, knowing that even though the world was imperfect and chaotic at the moment, things would change for the better. She could feel it in her bones.

This wasn't a fairy tale, not anywhere close. But she was starting to believe in happily ever after.

Liz DeJesus is the author of *The Jackets*, *The Frost Series*, *The Laurel*, *Girl*, *Mugshots*, *Zombie Ever After*, *ABC's with the Vejigantes*, and *The Shy Turtle*. Her work has also appeared in *Twice Upon a Time* and *Someone Wicked*. Her articles have been featured in *Southern Writers Magazine*. Liz won the 2023 Delaware Individual Artist Fellowship Emerging Professional in Literature: Creative Non-fiction. She was recently awarded the 2024 Artist Opportunity Grant from the Delaware Division of the Arts.